"Oh," I said. "Well, uh, what's your little girl's name?"

"Sunflower Moonbeam."

"I don't believe you."

She grinned. "I'm relieved you didn't bite on that one. I'm not *that* burnt-out an old hippie. Her name's Malinda. Mal for short."

"You're just saying that."

"No—it's true."

"That's nice. That's sweet."

"You never *really* forgave me, did you, Mal?"

"For what?"

"You know."

I knew.

"I tried," I said.

"I cut you too deep, didn't I?"

"I guess."

"I'm sorry."

"I know."

"I'm glad I got to see you again."

"I am too."

"I'm just in Iowa City, you know. We should see each other more often."

"We should. Let's make a point of it."

A month later, and she was dead.

Look for these other Tor books by Max Allan Collins

THE BABY BLUE RIP-OFF
NO CURE FOR DEATH
KILL YOUR DARLINGS
A SHROUD FOR AQUARIUS

A SHROUD
FOR AQUARIUS

MAX ALLAN COLLINS

TOR

A TOM DOHERTY ASSOCIATES BOOK

A SHROUD FOR AQUARIUS

Copyright © 1985 by Max Allan Collins

Reprinted by arrangement with The Walker Publishing Company, Inc.

First Tor Edition: June 1988

A TOR Book

Published by Tom Doherty Associates, Inc.
49 West 24 Street
New York, N.Y. 10010

ISBN: 0-812-50163-2
CAN. ED.: 0-812-50164-0

Printed in the United States of America

0 9 8 7 6 5 4 3 2 1

The portions of this novel pertaining to gaming and Las Vegas could not have been written without the advice and help of Charlie Stump, formerly of the Four Queens; the author's friend Chuck Mosser; and the author's father, Max A. Collins, Sr. Thank you, gentlemen.

M.A.C.

In memory of my good friend
Terry Beckey
who shared his music and laughter

1

I DON'T REMEMBER WHERE I WAS WHEN I HEARD President Kennedy was shot. It's a bench mark of my (and several) generations, I know; but I just don't remember, exactly. I know I was in junior high at the time, in one of my classes, and it came over the intercom; but which class, and what time of day, and who was sitting next to me, and other such specifics have faded from memory. Sorry.

On the other hand, I doubt I'll ever forget the moment when I heard Ginnie Mullens was shot. No one in my (or any) generation, other than the few of us who knew her, would ever consider that a bench mark of any kind. But I can tell you this: till senility or sudden death takes me, I'll remember that moment—frozen in my memory, like the proverbial fly in amber—when I heard about Ginnie dying.

I met Ginnie when we were both in diapers; the exact circumstances of that meeting are *not* frozen in my memory. I just know that our mothers were the best of friends, and Ginnie and I were inflicted upon each other at an early age. Neither of us could remember earlier than knowing each other.

For a long time—perhaps till age ten or eleven—we cheerfully hated each other. Ginnie was a tomboy of sorts, and considered me a sissy—I didn't like climbing trees with her, or shooting her B-B gun, either. She liked to play with a train set bequeathed to her by her older brother, and I was bored to tears with it.

"What's the point?" I asked her, both of us nine. "It just goes round and round."

"Does it have to have a point?" she asked me.

I thought about it.

"Yeah," I said. "I sort of think it does."

She gave me a Bronx cheer, despite the fact that we were in Port City, Iowa, and pushed the control and made the train go faster.

But we didn't play trains much after that, and a few years later, when we were a worldly thirteen, she copped to the fact that I'd made her think. I'd forgotten the incident, and wouldn't be able to report it now if she hadn't reminded me of it then.

"You got me to thinking," she said. "That things should have a point."

I shrugged. At thirteen I was well aware that life had a point: girls. (Ginnie, however, wasn't one of them: although an oddly "cute" girl with red hair and freckles and a nice little shape, I never considered her for romance. And she likewise never considered me in that fashion. We were more like brother and sister. Friends. We'd played doctor at age eight and that had been the extent of it. Once in a great while, when adolescent insomnia struck, I'd realize that seeing Ginnie without her britches at age thirteen just might be a different experience than at age eight. But then I'd feel guilty, somehow, and let it go.)

"And I don't mean girls," she said.

We were outside, sitting under a black sky full of silver stars. It was ten o'clock, but on a Friday night we could get away with it. Ginnie and her mom sometimes stayed over on the weekends. Years later I found out the reason.

"What *do* you mean?"

"Life. What's the point of it all? And is there a God? We go to Sunday school, but I think that's just social, don't you?"

I hadn't really thought about it. And that launched the first of many a soul-searching, existential discussion between Ginnie and me over the years. She had caught a fever I'd contracted a lot earlier on: reading. I was just graduating from the Hardy Boys into

Ellery Queen. But Ginnie had discovered Ayn Rand, and pretty soon we both decided we were objectivists. And deists. Both conditions, like our complexions, cleared up.

Then in junior high I decided I didn't just want to *read* books, I wanted to *write* them; and for a long time Ginnie was the only person I'd ever show my stories to, and after I went public in the ninth grade she remained my self-professed "biggest fan." She even typed the manuscripts I sent out in the mail (until I made it through a high school typing class myself) and provided me with inevitable moral support upon their inevitable rejection.

She had her own cockeyed goals, or at least so they seemed then. Women's lib was barely a rumor around these parts at the time; but Ginnie took such rumors seriously. She *knew* she would be a career woman—if not a professional, like a doctor or lawyer, then a *business*woman; not an employee, but an employ*er*—she wanted to be a millionaire by her thirtieth birthday. I didn't see why she couldn't—she was a brilliant student and a shrewd manipulator of those about her, with a wheeler-dealer's knack for getting her own way—and, anyway, it seemed like she was allowing herself plenty of time. . . .

We were good, good friends, as only a boy and a girl who are not romantically inclined toward each other can be. We shared books (in high school I turned her on to James M. Cain, and she showed me Albert Camus, and we both figured out the connection) and problems (though a conflict of interests arose when she was going with my best friend John in high school) and at church camp we gave Holy Hell to the poor ministers who were serving as counselors (still in our deist period).

At church camp one year we ran into a Born-Again–style minister who called the kids down from the pews to the front of the church to be saved. Neither Ginnie nor I went down there, and afterward one of our counselors questioned why—did the spirit not move us? Like any good fourteen-year-old male, I said, "I dunno." Ginnie said, "Just because I live in Iowa doesn't mean I have to moo my way to the cattle trough of faith." I still remember the pale look on the poor startled minister's face. He was just a kid, probably twenty-two; at the time I figured him to be ancient. Ginnie tested his faith, all right.

But she had more in mind that summer than just setting ministers straight about religion. She had met some dark-haired, dark-eyed kid from Lone Tree, a fifteen-year-old, and they went down to the lake and necked at night. Caused quite a sensation. I kissed a girl myself that year. Full-scale necking was out of my league, though: we were caught up in the last innocent throes of the *American Graffiti* years—the sexual revolution, where teenagers were concerned, was just a skirmish at this point. Ginnie, however, was there when they fired the first shot.

I may be the only person, outside of her parents, who knew about the abortion her junior year—at that time, that is. Later on she'd mention it rather freely, ostensibly as an example of the need for sex education in the schools, but in reality just to be shocking. She liked to shock. She'd liked to goose you with words, ideas, fancies.

We sat in the dark that night, and I held her. It was the first time since early adolescence that I'd felt anything like a romantic or remotely sexual stirring toward her. She told me she wanted to have the baby, but her parents talked her out of it.

"Is it murder?" she asked.

"I don't think so," I said, not sure.

"It isn't a person. Not yet. It's just a fetus."

"You're right."

"I don't think abortion's wrong, Mal. Or evil. Do you?"

"No."

"I wish you'd say 'no' like you meant it."

"I wish I could, too. I wish I could give you some support. But this is new to me."

"Jeez, Mal, it's new to me, too!"

"Ginnie, I never even *slept* with a girl, and you want advice from me on ..."

"Abortion. Abortion. Abortion. Say it, Mal."

"Abortion."

"I'm too young to be a mother."

"You're pretty mature for your age, though."

"In what sense?"

I shrugged. "Most every sense."

"So, what? You think I should have the kid?"

"I don't know."

"We're not *Catholics*, you know. We're Methodists!"

"And not very Methodist, if you get right down to it."

"Right. I'm not having it."

"The abortion?"

"The baby! Oh, Mal, can't you be of more help than this? You're just pitiful...."

"I'm sorry, Ginnie."

"It isn't John's, you know."

"Well, I figured. You broke up and all."

"I don't want to tell you whose it is."

"That's okay."

" 'Cause I'm not going to have this baby."

"Hey, I'm on your side."

She smiled and looked at me. Her freckles were washed out by the moonlight. "You really are, aren't you? Whatever I decide is okay with you."

"Sure. What are friends for?"

She started to sing a Carole King song, then: "When you're down and troubled ..."

She didn't have a very good voice, but it was moving, hearing her sing that, her thin voice cracking every fourth word or so. I held her hand. We sat. I held her. She cried. I didn't cry till I got home. I didn't think crying in front of her was the sort of support she needed.

* * *

We drifted apart our senior year. Drugs had hit the Iowa high schools, about two years after it hit the two coasts (there was a time lag then that has been reduced from years to weeks now), and Ginnie was into them heavily. Grass was just the beginning; she smoked hash, dropped acid, went the whole hallucinogenic route. She and a group of girls were the school hippies in their beads and tie-dyed clothes, and became combination outcasts and celebrities.

Me, I was very uptight about drugs. I was involved in sports and wanted nothing to do with those substances. A year later I'd be in Vietnam smoking dope, and not long after that in Haight Ashbury doing drugs Ginnie had never *heard* of back in high school; but at the moment, I was a virgin and possessed a smug righteousness about my chemical celibacy.

"Loosen up," she said, lighting up a joint in my parents' rec room.

"I don't go for that shit," I said.

"Come on! You listen to the *Beatles*, don't you?"

"Yeah, but I hate the White Album. Now, don't *do* that in here! My parents are upstairs, for Christ's sake. And so's your mom."

"What's she going to do about it?"

Ginnie's mom was a wonderful person, but she had about as much control over Ginnie as ... as I did.

"You shouldn't do that to yourself," I said.

"It's *mind*-expanding, Mal. Christ! After all the long philosophical raps we had over the years on the meaning of life, and you reject the *key*."

"If that's the key, I got no interest in the door. I hate that smell."

"You are a drag. I never thought I'd see the day. But you are a drag, Mal. A real drag. A drag."

"Let me see if I've got this straight. I'm a drag."

"Straight is right. A drag."

I didn't see much of her after that, our senior year. Except for one disastrous encounter in the cafeteria, perhaps a month later.

I sat down with my tray of food across from Ginnie. Several of my friends joined me. Male friends. Guys I played football with, played cards with. Ginnie was sitting with two of her hippie girl friends; cute girls, one of whom was dating one of the guys who'd sat down with me.

We began chatting about various school matters. I mentioned I was working on a short story to be entered in a national competition.

Ginnie snorted. "That's a laugh."

"Pardon?"

"Mal, you're such an unimaginative pathetic little shit, what could *you* write?"

I felt as though someone had hit me hard in the stomach; I could feel the discomfort of my friends next to me, despite their nervous smiles.

I wasn't smiling when I pointed my finger at Ginnie like a gun.

"We're through," I told her. "We've been friends for a long time, but we're through. It's over."

She laughed. Her girl friends laughed.

I stood. "Was putting me down for laughs worth our friendship? I hope so. Because I'm never speaking to you again."

She laughed some more, but in her eyes I could see what I'd said had registered.

And as the weeks, the months went by, she would approach me and grin and say, "Still mad?" And I wouldn't speak. When my story won the national competition, she came up and congratulated me and I said nothing, feeling no sense of victory, just empty. Finally, at the all-night party after the senior prom, a party held on a *Delta Queen*–style riverboat that lurched down the Mississippi while a rock band played "Louie Louie" so many times we eventually thought we could understand the words, she approached me with tears in her eyes and said, only, "Can we be friends again?"

And I said, sure.

But it was never the same again.

I ran into her over the summer, several times, but there was a strain and the conversation remained polite, brittle. And pretty soon I went to Vietnam, and she went to the university, pre-law.

Two years later I was in an army hospital, Stateside, and her letter found its way to me;

in it she said: "It's New Year's Eve. I don't usually write letters, Mal—I guess you know that. But tonight, for some reason, I have to deal with what I did to you in the cafeteria that time. I hurt you. I don't know why I said what I did—strike that. I do know. It's the gambler in me, the risk taker; more than that—that nihilistic streak of mine. I knew what our relationship meant—and I decided to see what would happen if I—just—mindlessly—*lashed out* at you. Just to see what would happen. And I saw. I ruined us. Can you forgive me?"

I was moved that she would—after all this time—write such a note. And I wrote back: "Of course, I forgive you. What are friends for?"

Yet even then, something was gone. Because over the years, that cafeteria incident remained between us, somehow. She lived in Iowa City—not forty miles from me, who lived in Port City, our home town, where I settled after my bouts with Vietnam and Haight Ashbury. She ran a head shop up there, ever since dropping out of law school. Even at the peak of her hippie period she never let go of her make-a-million-by-thirty goal. From the looks of her shop, maybe she'd made it: Ginnie's ETC., ETC., ETC., was more than just a head shop, having grown from a hole-in-the-wall storefront to a three-story building downtown: she sold furniture and lamps and what-have-you for apartment dwellers, which a college town like Iowa City has more than its share of. But the dope paraphernalia remained a part of the shop, and I had—post-Vietnam/Haight Ashbury—gone celibate where dope was concerned, and had a passionate disinterest in it. Full circle. A virgin again.

Still, whenever I was in Iowa City, I'd stop in the shop and say hello. Now and then she would call me on the phone, just to talk—once it was to see if I was as angry that NBC had cancelled "SCTV" as she was. I was. We decided to make phone calls and write letters of protest. We felt close again. Closer than in years, and over the phone.

A few years of no contact drifted by. The last time I saw her was at our fifteenth high school class reunion, the month before. She was happy, she said. Business was good, she said, though she had not made her million yet; what the hell, goals were made to be ignored. Or anyway, adjusted. Was money still her *main* goal? She shrugged. What about her personal life? She was married and had a little girl, four years old.

"I still think John was the love of my life," she said. "Sometimes at night I still think of him. And cry a little."

John was killed in Vietnam.

"Me too," I said.

She was wearing layered clothing, earth tones. She had on a clunky, funky necklace. She still had her nice little shape, her freckles, her red hair in an attractive shag. "I wish you could see my little girl," she said.

"I'd love to. Who's staying with her?"

"She's with her daddy."

"I haven't seen J.T. for a long time."

She shrugged. "We're separated."

"Oh," I said. "Well, uh, what's your little girl's name?"

"Sunflower Moonbeam."

"I don't believe you."

She grinned. "I'm relieved you didn't bite on that one. I'm not *that* burnt-out an old hippie. Her name's Malinda. Mal for short."

"You're just saying that."

"No—it's true."

"That's nice. That's sweet."

"You never *really* forgave me, did you, Mal?"

"For what?"

"You know."

I knew.

"I tried," I said.

"I cut you too deep, didn't I?"

"I guess."

"I'm sorry."

"I know."

"I'm glad I got to see you again."

"I am too."

"I'm just in Iowa City, you know. We should see each other more often."

"We should. Let's make a point of it."

A month later, and she was dead.

2

THE PHONE RANG ME AWAKE.

He must've let it ring twenty times or I would have just worked it into my dream and ignored it; but finally I was shuffling out of bed, glancing at the fluorescent hands of the little round clock on my nightstand, heading for the phone, grumbling.

"Y-yes?" I said. My voice must've sounded as thick as my mouth felt.

"Mallory, sorry to wake you. It's Sheriff Brennan."

"Brennan?"

"Yeah. Sorry. Look uh—I got a situation, here, and—"

"It's three o'clock in the fucking morning!"

There was a pause, then: "Do you eat with that mouth?"

I tasted my tongue. "Maybe not, from here on out." My brain was gradually sending me the signal that Brennan wouldn't be calling at this hour unless it was an emergency. I waited for him to confirm that suspicion.

He did: "A friend of yours is dead. Little Ginnie Mullens."

The phone sits in a recess in the wall in the nook that joins the bedroom, office, bathroom, and dining room of my small house. By the phone, there's a chair. I sat in it.

"Mallory?"

I sighed. "I heard you."

"You don't seem very—surprised."

"I haven't had time to get around to that yet."

"Shot in the head."

"Oh, no."

"Looks to be a suicide."

"Aw, shit."

"I thought you'd want to know."

"I—I do. Uh. Thank you for calling."

"She was a friend of my son's, you know."

Brennan was the father of my late friend John. Who'd died in Vietnam. Who'd been Ginnie's high school sweetheart.

"Yeah. I know. Brennan?"

"Yeah?"

"This could've waited till morning."

"Yeah, suppose it could've."

"I'm not giving you a hard time for calling—I appreciate it and everything. But why didn't you wait till morning?"

He cleared his throat. Brennan's not the type to get nervous; he's a big man in his fifties who has been sheriff of Port County for as long as I can remember. The kind of sheriff who wears a Stetson hat and gets away with it.

But he seemed awkward, even nervous, now.

He said, "Thought you'd rather hear it from me."

I smiled. This was no time to be smiling, and maybe that was *my* nerves. But Brennan and I had never gotten along really well; not when John and I were friends in high school, or even when we went to Vietnam on the buddy system together, or especially when I came home and was a long-haired vet actively against the war. Especially not then.

My hair was shorter now, and I was a respectable citizen. I wrote books. Didn't make a fortune at it, but was no longer just a scruffy guy living in a trailer on East Hill who talked about wanting to write. I was a clean-shaven "author" who lived in a house. More a bungalow, but anyway not a trailer, though still on East Hill.

Yeah, I'd arrived. I was straight again, and down on drug use, and up with people, and all the square things Ginnie had made fun of me for when we were drifting apart our senior year in high school.

"Are you okay, kid?"

I wasn't a kid anymore, either, but somehow I liked hearing Brennan call me that—

over the phone at least. It was comforting, in some weird way. I wiped the wetness off my face with my hand and wiped my hand on my T-shirt.

I said, "Let's not kid each other. You don't think enough of me to do me any favors, Brennan. What's this about?"

There was another long pause. Another clearing of his throat. And then a forced laugh.

"Yeah, well, I know we've had our bad moments. But you were my son's friend, and—"

"Brennan. What?"

"I'm still at the scene."

"The scene?"

"Of the crime."

"Crime? You said it was suicide."

"Suicide's a crime, ain't it?"

"Suicide sounds like the sort of case you could solve even without my help."

"Let's not bicker, son."

Hearing him call me "son" sent a lump to my throat. I couldn't tell you why.

But I said, "Sorry. That was uncalled for."

"Yeah, it was. How would you like to come out here?"

It was a farmhouse on a blacktop just off Highway 22, just past West Liberty. A big, stark white two-story with gothic lines set in a valley between two hills, sitting against a clear, starry summer sky. In the daytime this country looked like Grant Wood had painted it, and the farmhouse might've been the one his couple with the stern expressions and pitchfork posed in front of. At night it was just a farmhouse, and in the moonlight the rich rolling hills looked a barren gray. The only color was provided by the ambulance pulled into the graveled drive, its cherrytop turning and painting all in its path red, as two young men were loading a covered stretcher into the back. I got out of my car and walked over.

Big Brennan, badge pinned to the light summer jacket over his cream-colored shirt, stood with his hands on his hips, gunbutt jutting, and pushed his Stetson back on his head, smiling tightly at me. He brushed a well-greased lock of brown hair off his lined forehead. He looked like a Marlboro man, only he didn't smoke.

"Nice of you to come."

"Nice of you to ask."

There was an awkward moment. Twice over the last eight years I'd been involved in murder cases that Brennan had handled. I am by no stretch of the imagination a detective, professional or amateur or anything else. My writing has dealt with crime, however, which is, I guess, the connection. Anyway, those two times, Brennan had been less than hospitable to my presence. Understandably. I was a civilian, getting in the way.

On the other hand, I had proved unexpectedly helpful in both instances. And the last of the two instances—a couple of years ago—

had left Brennan and me in a state of uneasy truce.

Still, what was I doing here?"

"Brennan," I said, "what am I *doing* here?"

He shrugged, blew some air out, like he'd been underwater holding his breath for five or ten minutes. He grinned at me whitely; the grin I remembered—the teeth seemed to be new.

"Nice car," he said.

I looked at the ambulance, the back of which was being shut by the two ambulance guys, both of whom I knew; they worked for the local funeral home but did emergency calls for the living as well. Would that tonight fell in the latter category.

"What car?" I asked. I tucked my hands in my jeans pockets; there was a light, sweet-smelling summer breeze.

"What do you think?" he said, smiling on one side of his face, cracking his tan. "Those are pretty fancy wheels."

"Oh," I said.

He meant *my* car—a silver Firebird.

"Just like Rockford drives," he said.

"Brennan, they canceled that show, all right? Did you ask me here at four in the morning to talk about my car and old TV?"

Then I saw that the smiles were all a facade. He was shaken, this tough old bird. His blue eyes—my friend John's blue eyes stuck in his father's skull—were watery. The small talk was just Brennan working out his nerves, and hiding how he really felt.

"Let's step inside," he said.

I moved toward the ambulance. "I want to say goodbye to Ginnie, first. Bill? Can you open that back up again?"

Bill, a thin kid in his twenties who also worked at the local movie house, swallowed, glanced at his heavyset partner, Fred; Bill's mouth, and the unlikely Gable mustache above it, twitched. "Sure, Mal. If you were a friend of the deceased, I don't see why not."

I took a step, then felt Brennan's hand on my shoulder.

He whispered in my ear. "Say goodbye from here." His breath smelled like Clorets.

Bill stood poised by the doors, a hand on one handle.

"It's okay, Bill," I said, waving him off. "Thanks anyway."

Bill nodded, and got in the ambulance and went away. No siren. What for?

I watched it glide up the hill and disappear over the top and said, to myself, " 'Bye, Ginnie."

Then I followed Brennan into the house.

We went in the front way and were in a high-ceilinged living room; it was an odd mixture of eras. Pastels, earth tones, dominated. Most of the furniture was antique, including an oak ice-chest turned into a liquor cabinet. Plants in pots grew on window ledges and on the floor in corners and climbed up the edge of the second-floor steps. But there were several pieces of modern furniture, including a geometric couch with brown and tan interchangeable elements and the odd art deco piece, a lamp of a nude woman holding a ball of light, another that was a rounded airplane out of a thirties Disney cartoon, glowing orange. There was a 26" Sony color TV and a component stereo against one wall; no bookcase. The floor was plushly carpeted, wall to wall, in a tan shag. And on the walls were framed art nouveau prints. It was an interior decorator's nightmare, particularly because it worked.

"She had a nice life here," Brennan said, glancing around.

It didn't matter that the things in this room were largely of no interest to him: that they had cost plenty of money impressed him. That made Ginnie's life "nice," by definition. His.

"She sure did."

He pointed. "She, uh—did it upstairs."

We went up past the plants to the top of the stairs and a small room, three walls of which were lined with books. Books of all kinds. Book by Buckminster Fuller, Aldous Huxley, John Lily, Timothy Leary, Carlos Castaneda. *Bury My Heart At Wounded Knee. The Great Gatsby. Eleven Kinds of Loneliness.* A few paperback mysteries I'd given her back in junior high, stacked together: Hammett, Chandler, Spillane, Roscoe Kane. Two books called *Casino Gambling*, one by Feinman, another by Barnhart. Other gambling books by Goren and Scharff. Books by Albert Camus, James M. Cain. And some schmuck called Mallory.

There was a desk by a window, an old beat-up rolltop that had belonged to her father, the top rolled up. Various scattered papers, soaked with blood. The window seemed smeared with something.

"She did it here at this desk?" I asked.

"That's how it looks," Brennan said.

"Any note?"

"None. Those papers are some kind of figuring. Arithmetic."

"Who found her?"

"We did. People in the farmhouse across the way called it in. Heard gunfire."

"Tell me more."

He shrugged. "She was slumped there. Was, uh—wasn't wearing nothing. Gun in her hand, bullet through her brain." He swallowed; trying to say it brusquely didn't seem to have done the trick for him. "It was worse than that, really. It was a big gun—.357 mag. Wasn't much of her head left."

That's why he hadn't wanted me to see her.

I looked around the desk. "Where's the, uh—"

"Brain matter and such? We cleaned it up already." He nodded toward the smeary window. There was a splintery hole, from the bullet apparently, in the wood. "We're 'bout done here. My two punk deputies have taken pictures of the scene and all."

"Where are they now?"

"Having a look around the rest of the house, steppin' on each other's peckers, more'n likely."

"What are they looking for?"

He shrugged again. "Drugs, maybe."

"Drugs," I said flatly.

"That's right." He pointed to the book shelf; his finger lit on *The Teachings of Don Juan.* "I hate to think it about little Ginnie, but there's no getting around it. She was a hippie."

"That term's a little out of date, isn't it?"

"Is it?" he said, sniffing the air.

Which smelled like incense.

There was a small brass burner cut with Indian designs near the blood-soaked papers. There was also an ashtray and a half-smoked joint.

"I guess she never completely got over being a hippie," I said.

"Well, I hear she was a capitalistic sort of hippie."

"I guess you could say that. Her business in Iowa City was successful, certainly."

"I didn't mean that."

I looked at him sharply. "What *did* you mean?"

"I got friends on the Iowa City department."

"Street sweeping?"

He grimaced. "Cops. Don't be cute, Mallory."

"Sorry. It's just my way of dealing with this. So you got friends on the Iowa City police force. So?"

He sat on the edge of the desk. "I called one of 'em tonight. Asked him if he knew of anything ... unusual, where Ginnie or her business was concerned."

"And? Spit it out, Brennan."

He sighed heavily. Weight of the world. "He says everybody knows that for years Ginnie dealt that shit." Nodding at the half-smoked joint. "And worse. There's one of them coke mirrors downstairs."

I thought about Ginnie dealing. That was possible. I thought about her still doing dope, including cocaine. That was also possible. Somehow it made me even sadder than I already was.

"Let's get out of this room," I said.

"Just a second," he said. "I want to show you something."

He knelt; pointed to a scorched hole, bigger than a dime, smaller than a quarter, in the oriental rug.

"See that?" he said. "It's another bullet hole."

I got down and looked. "Yeah, it is."

"Now, I'm sure when we check her out, Ginnie's going to have fired a gun—specifically that big mother we found in her hand. But why'd she shoot twice? Once in the floor, then in her head?"

Still crouching, scratching my chin, I said, "Maybe to work up the courage?"

He nodded, rising. "Maybe."

I rose, too. "Or maybe somebody shot her in the head, put the gun in her hand and fired off another round, so tests'd show she'd fired the thing."

He nodded some more, slowly now.

"I can see why this strikes you as possibly murder," I said, poking toward the bullet hole in the floor with my foot. "It isn't overwhelming, but it raises some doubt."

"Let me ask you something else," he said, going to one of the bookcases. "What's all *this* about?"

He pointed to the shelf of gambling books.

I half smiled. "Ginnie was a gambler, didn't you know that?"

He shook his head no.

"She worked as a blackjack dealer in Tahoe and Vegas during her college years, summers. Long as I knew her, she used to go to Vegas every now and then."

"A hippie in Vegas?"

"Consistency is the hobgoblin of the small mind. Or something."

"Who said that?"

"I don't remember. Ginnie could've told you, though."

He glanced around at the walls of books. "Bet she could." Cleared his throat. "Let's get out of here."

We walked by the plants down the stairs back into the living room. I sat on the modernistic couch, but Brennan paced. A big, nervous cat.

"Trouble is," he said, "I ain't equipped to do a murder investigation."

"*Is* this a murder investigation?"

"No," he said. "That's the trouble."

"Explain."

He wandered over to the stack of stereo equipment in a dark wood rack; there was a lava lamp on one of the speakers, with red flowing, bubbling in it, an anachronistic reminder of who Ginnie had been ten or more years ago. And who I had been.

Studying the flowing red, he said, "This goes down as suicide. I'm suspicious, but there's not enough to view it any other way. If I had a little more, I could ask the Port City department in on it. Or, better, the State Division of Criminal Investigation."

"I'm surprised this is your jurisdiction at all."

He smirked. "It barely is. We're half a mile from the county line. I'm not set up to handle a murder case; all I got are a couple of young punk deputies, so wet behind the ears their brains are soggy—my budget's been cut to shit, last few years. Hell. Iowa City'd be better handling this, considering they got some plainclothes staff and those boys has got their suspicions about Ginnie in general."

"Are you going to look into it? Or write it off as suicide?"

"I'm going to talk to the county coroner. Ask him to schedule the inquest for a week from now."

"Why so long?"

"To give you time."

I put my hand on my chest, like I was swearing on oath. "Me? Shit! Why me?"

He sat next to me, put a hand on my knee, smiled at me like an insurance agent. "You knew Ginnie. You're her age. You had the same friends."

"Yeah. Fifteen years ago. So?"

"So ask around about her. In Iowa City. In Port City. See if you hear anything, pick up anything . . . anything that's at all . . . *interesting*. Then come to me. If it's anything at *all*, I'll go to the D.C.I. with it."

I shook my head. "I don't believe this. You're *asking* me to play detective? With your blessing?"

He scowled. "*Not* play detective. Just ask around. And not with my blessing. This is off the record. I'm looking the other way, is all."

"Why are you doing this?"

He swallowed. His eyes were wet. Blinking, he said, "Ginnie loved my boy, once upon a time. And he loved her, once upon a time. She was a sweet girl. If . . . if he hadn't gone off to war, maybe they'd have got married out of high school, maybe she'd have straightened out and I'd have grandkids and both her and John'd be alive tonight. Maybe."

We sat there for a while; there were some sounds out in the kitchen. The deputies, looking.

I said, "Maybe you're right." I meant right about John and Ginnie both being alive today, if they'd stayed together and the world had gone a different way. But I also meant right about this being murder. Brennan took it both ways.

"I'm right," he said.

"And maybe you can't accept that little Ginnie Mullens could kill herself."

He stood. "No! Can you? Alive, vital, curious, smart. Pretty little vivacious thing like her. Can you?"

I shook my head. "Not really. She was also very selfish. She liked life, wrung every last experience out of it. *I* can't make myself believe it, either."

"I didn't think so."

"But I haven't seen much of her in recent years. She could've changed."

"Ask around. Find out if she did."

I stood. Wandered over to the lava lamp. Touched it; it was warm, almost hot. I kept my hand there. "I'd like to know, Brennan. If she did kill herself, I'd like to know why. If she didn't—and I'm with you, I don't think she did—I'd like to know who *did* kill her, and why. And, I'd like to see whoever did it check into a suite down at the Fort Madison pen for life."

Brennan smiled. "I hear prison conditions down there ain't so good."

"Generally I'm all for prison reform," I said. "But I'd send whoever killed Ginnie to Devil's Island, if I could."

He stood, hitched his trousers, walked over like John Wayne and put a hand on my shoulder. He liked hearing a supposed liberal like me talk like a raving conservative. "What do you say, son?"

I gave him something that felt like a smile. "Sure. I'll ask around for you. John would want me to."

He nodded.

"You tell her mother yet?"

He shook his head no, looking at the floor. "Why wake her in the middle of the night for it? It'll keep. She'll be miserable soon enough. I did call the husband, though. He lives in Davenport with the child."

"How'd he take it?"

"Hard to say. His voice was real quiet. Thanked me for calling. That was about it. He'll have to break it to the little girl himself, poor bastard. As for Ginnie's mom, I'll call on her, personal. First thing tomorrow morning."

"I don't envy you."

"It's what they pay me for."

"I never thought I'd say this, Brennan, but whatever they're paying you, it's not enough."

"I never thought I'd be saying this, Mallory, but for once I agree with you."

A young deputy came in from the kitchen; he had flour on his hands. "I been through everything. Didn't find no drugs."

"Nice work," Brennan said sourly, then smiled wryly at me.

I nodded to Brennan and went out into the cool July night. Morning, actually. I looked up at the sky and thought about the nights

I'd spent sitting out with Ginnie, looking up at the stars.

Then I got in my car and headed home, the thought of finding out the truth about her violent death holding back the tears.

3

IT WAS A NEW BUILDING DOING ITS BEST TO seem old. Funky old; hip old; chic old. A red-brick, three-story building with a glass face, trimmed in tarnished metal, letters of which spelled out ETC., ETC., ETC., above chrome-handled gray steel doors.

I had parked across the street, in the ramp adjacent to Old Capitol Center, an enclosed mall two tall stories high, a massive brown-brick building that swallowed a city block in one big bite. Old Cap Center tried to hide what it was by providing showroom windows like mock storefronts, though none of the mall's stores could be entered from the street, and most of the showroom windows were empty, giving Old Cap a vaguely institutional look—a mall in a police state. It

31

faced real storefronts across the way, including all three ETC.'s.

I crossed the street. Directly before me (around the corner from ETC.'s, which was to my left) was an open plaza, where two block-long rows of boutiques and trendy little restaurants faced each other across a street closed off to traffic. That street made a T, a block down, with another similarly closed-off street, both streets walkways now, pavement replaced with brick, sidewalk vendors selling pretzels and popcorn, railroad-tie benches and planters and trees perching where cars once parked, students and the occasional native Iowa Citian strolling where cars might once have cheerfully run them down. There was a fountain in the midst of what had been the intersection, including a modern art sculpture (unless that was just the final auto mishap from before the streets were closed off, left there to rust). Nearby, too, was a playground area where kids attempted to make sense out of the rope and wood devices that had supplanted such cruel capitalistic contrivances as swings and slides. The whole of downtown Iowa City—having undergone a recent urban renewal—was earth tones, natural as a salad with sprouts. Former hippies were on the Chamber of Commerce, now, and they had built a little utopia for their heirs, the preppies and the punks.

More preppies than punks, though, and not that many of either on this pleasantly warm day. Maybe it was the hour (ten o'clock in the morning) and the time of year (summer school was in session) but Iowa City was relatively deserted. Still, in the generously wide brick crosswalk, I encountered two boys in shirts with little alligators on their pockets, a girl in a light short-sleeve cardigan with a Hawkeye pin, another boy in a yellow and gold "Go Hawks" tank top, a girl in a mohawk and a torn Dead Kennedys T-shirt, walking with a boy in a black leather vest with a backward swastika graffitied on. I figured his swastika and her Dead Kennedys (a punk-rock band) had about as much to do with these kids' politics as the alligators and hawks did the others. I wore apparel decorated neither with reptiles nor Nazi symbols, or birds of prey, either; a member of the first television generation, I wore a T-shirt on which was a picture of Phil Silvers as Sgt. Bilko, the green lettering of which matched my camouflage gym shorts.

The glass facade of ETC., ETC., ETC., looked right in on the main floor. I was somewhat surprised to discover, entering, that it was now devoted to food; once upon a time this had been the head shop area. Now it was cookware, cookbooks, coffee makers and such, with a section of imported foods, particularly pastas, and at the right a bakery counter, currently sending the scent of croissants to mingle with the smell of various exotic coffees sitting in squat bags before me like fat little people on shelves. Centerstage was a display case of expensive candy, and at right, toward the back, a small deli case with fancy cheeses and salamis. Behind all the counters were very well-groomed young men with short hair and tastefully "new wave" apparel. They all smiled at me. If I were a nice person, I'd figure 'em friendly; me, I figured 'em gay.

There were four other floors, or levels, linked by wide, gray, all-weather-carpeted, open stairways with black metal bannisters; the basement was a gift shop, running to those airbrushed cards of Betty Boop, movie stars, and hunky males, plus stationery, candles, jewelry, stuffed toys; the second floor was apartment furnishings, lots of pine and burlap cloth this year, and also some starkly modern steel office furniture painted bright reds and blacks; the third floor was women's apparel, looking expensive, imported, and rather humorless, but up the steps in the smaller, fourth-floor area was more women's clothing, vaguely new-wave-looking items. I checked a few of the tags on them, finding, next to prices that curled my hair, the names Norma Kamali and Betsy Johnson.

But I wasn't looking for Norma or Betsy. I was looking for Caroline.

She would most likely be on this fourth landing in a certain office marked EMPLOY-EES ONLY behind a certain counter. Also behind that counter was a nicely dressed young man in a rust polo shirt and tan slacks and short razor cut hair and a delicate thin mustache that seemed to have been cut a hair at a time. He smiled at me, till I went behind his counter and knocked on the door.

"Caroline doesn't want to be disturbed," he said.

"How do we know till we ask Caroline?"

The door opened and a short, thin, pale woman with hawkish features and severe short black hair that hooked around each side of her face like upside-down beaks, wearing a black pullover and black slacks and looking like Ayn Rand's photo on the jacket of one of the books Ginnie and I had read back in high school, said, "I don't care to be disturbed."

I shrugged at the nicely dressed young man. "You were right."

Caroline Westin's eyes narrowed, looking up past my Sgt. Bilko T-shirt, and she said, "You're Mallory, aren't you?"

"Right," I said, impressed. We'd only met once.

"We only met once," she said, showing me into her small, white, barely furnished office, "but Ginnie had a picture of the two of you on her desk in her office."

"No kidding?" I sat in a straightbacked chair as she got behind a gray metal desk, nothing fashionable like you could buy a floor down. "I was in her office before ... *this* office, actually, when it was hers. I never saw that picture."

She shrugged, lighting a cigarette in a black holder. "She probably hid it when she saw you coming. She wasn't much for showing how she really felt."

"From your use of the past tense, I take it you know about Ginnie. Her death."

"Yes. The sheriff in Port City called me not long ago."

"If you'll excuse me for saying it, you don't seem too shook up about it."

"I couldn't care less what you say or think," she said, with a smile so thin and curling it had to mean more to her than me, because I sure couldn't figure a meaning for a smile like that.

I said, "You were business partners for, what? Five or six years? And didn't you share a house here in town?"

She nodded, still smiling, the cigarette holder stuck in the thin, curling line of her smile like a catheter.

"So," I said, "one might expect a little show of grief."

"I don't give a damn what one might expect," she said, in a tone of voice that didn't give a damn what one might expect. And then sarcasm finally edged its way in: "However, why should the bereaved friend complain of anyone else's inappropriate show of mourning when he himself chooses to wear a grinning 1950s television personality, instead of black?"

She was in black, but I had a feeling that was her style, not out of respect.

"I deserved that," I said, smiling a little. "I found out about Ginnie last night. So I've

had a chance to adjust to it a little. And I'll
be honest with you. Ginnie and I weren't
close in recent years. I feel the loss, all right.
But when someone dies who once was close
to you—who was part of your daily life, once
upon a time, but who has long since *left* your
daily life, a fact to which you adjusted some
time ago—well, the loss just isn't as keenly
felt as it should be. As it would be should
someone from your current daily life happen
to die. I feel a little guilty about that. If
Ginnie had died fifteen years ago, it would've
shattered me. Today, it only saddens me.
Saddens, and ... confuses me."

My confession seemed to have embarrassed
her; her composure slipped, just a hair, as
she said, "I sympathize with your ... feel-
ings, Mr. Mallory. But if you're looking for
someone to ... bring you up to date where
Ginnie's concerned, to ... help you get to
know the person she became since *high
school*, well ... you'll just have to look
elsewhere."

"Who could know her better than her
business partner? Someone she shared a
house with, for Christ's sake?"

She stood, removing the cigarette from the
holder and stubbing it out, in what I read as
a surprising show of anger from a woman
whose face remained cool, pale, impenetrable.

She said, "I didn't say I didn't know her. I
knew her very well indeed. But I didn't like
her, Mr. Mallory. And you want to put your
head on someone's shoulder and have some-

one say, 'There, there,' and afterward put their head on your shoulder so you can say, 'There, there,' and generally be miserable together and purge whatever individual guilt you might feel in a mutual, sloppy show of sentiment, and that's *fine* . . . if you liked her. I didn't.''

Suddenly I knew something. Or at least thought I did.

"*You* did once," I said.

"What?" Her head jerked back, just a little.

"Like her. You liked her once."

She shrugged. "Sure. We were friendly." Her fingers searched the desk for her cigarettes, while her eyes looked at me with a cold searching stare. I reached over and pushed the cigarettes, Salems, into the path of her fingers.

"You lived together," I said.

She sat down. "We lived together, yes." She lit up again, but without the holder this time.

"Ginnie was an experimenter," I said. "With people as well as drugs. You were lovers, weren't you?"

She smoked for a while, deciding whether or not to answer.

Then she said, "We were for a while. But like most gamblers . . ." The enigmatic smile returned, seeming less enigmatic now. ". . . eventually she cheated."

"Who with?"

"Does it matter?"

"Just wondering."

She laughed mirthlessly, smoke curling out her nostrils, dragonlike. "You're a nosy little bastard."

"We all have our little quirks."

"You're a nasty little bastard, too."

"I didn't mean that to sound nasty," I said truthfully. "And I'm not shocked, or disapproving of your relationship with Ginnie. I feel a little naive for not figuring it out a long time ago, though."

She said, meaning to be nasty, I think, "You *were* born in Iowa, weren't you?"

"Yeah. There's no law against it. Some people are born *and* die here. Ginnie, for instance."

"It was that jerk she married."

"What?"

"That's who she cheated on me with. That hippie jerk she married."

"She didn't ever take his last name, did she?"

"No. She was independent, our Ginnie. His name was O'Hara. John O'Hara. The poet, not the novelist."

"Didn't he sign his work J.T. O'Hara?"

"That's right. Didn't want to be confused with a *real* writer, I would guess."

"That's a little cruel, isn't it?"

"Have you ever read any of his poetry?"

Actually, I had; but she still struck me as cruel, grain of truth in it or not.

I said, "I understand Ginnie's daughter's living with O'Hara."

She nodded. Then she smirked to herself, reflecting. "Her most recent romantic conquest was Iowa City's resident media guru."

"David Flater," I said, nodding. "Ginnie mentioned him to me when I saw her last."

"Ginnie used people," she said. Finally opening up. "She used me. I was a business major, getting top grades. But I ran in what you might call *counter-culture* circles. I found approval with Ginnie, J.T., the rest of them. The last gasp of the hippie generation. Ha. But I knew this college life was . . . fleeting. And I feared the approval of Ginnie and the others would be something I wouldn't find out there, in the . . . real world. Some of my personal habits might've gotten in the way when I went to find a job in the straight world, I thought—wrongly, I now believe. I could've adjusted. With my brains, my ambition, my skills, my talent, I could've made it *anywhere.*"

What this woman needed was a little self-confidence.

"But Ginnie seduced me, in more ways than one. I came in, here at ETC.'s, as her business associate, a glorified bookkeeper, really. Then when my father died and I inherited some money, she gave me the glorious opportunity to buy into this little gold mine. Ha! I didn't know she'd been on her good behavior that first year—that before I came aboard, she'd salted away enough fun money to hold her awhile. It was later I found how she'd pull money out of the

business on a whim—to go to Vegas, to play
the market, even here in the store to buy
some line of goods that she figured would
take off. . . ."

"Wasn't she pretty smart about that sort of
thing? I remember she was the first to show
Tiffany-style lamp shades around here, and
before that turquoise jewelry . . . she must've
made a mint at both—"

She shrugged, granting me that. "But she
just as often struck out. She bought a truckload of pink flamingoes, a few years ago,
because it was a kitsch sort of thing; she
figured that John Waters cult movie and the
new-wave influence and all that would hit
here and make those plastic birds the talk of
the town. We ended up having to dump 'em
to a flea market merchant at an eighty
percent loss. Iowa City doesn't know kitsch
from a kitchen sink. This town's hipper than
Port City, but SoHo it ain't."

"So you bought her out. Two months
ago?" Ginnie had mentioned, at our high
school reunion last month, that her partner
Caroline Westin had taken over the business.

And right now Caroline Westin was smiling, a flared-nostril sort of smile that didn't
have anything to do with good humor. "You're
goddamn right I bought her out two months
ago. With what was left of my inheritance,
and what I'd saved and made investing from
my own share of this place. I wanted her *out*
of here. First thing I did was move out that

goddamn head shop crap. That's *yesterday,* and it's dangerous, besides."

"Too much local legislation against selling drug paraphernalia, you mean."

"That's right, and it's lousy for the image. We have college-kid clientele here, certainly, but mostly it's grad students and teachers and lawyers and doctors and professional people in general—yesterday, this place served Yippies. We're into Yuppies now. Got it?"

"Got it."

"It's not that some of our clientele aren't into drugs. I'm sure some marijuana is still being smoked, and some cocaine is certainly being snorted. But they don't buy their furniture, or their Kamali clothes, or their goddamn *pasta,* at the same place they purchase rolling papers and coke mirrors."

"Was Ginnie still dealing dope?"

Her pale face went suddenly paler. Her mouth a slash, her eyes stones. "No drug dealing's been connected to ETC., ETC., ETC., *ever.*"

"That's not what I asked."

She stood up. "Why don't you leave?"

I smiled, gestured in a peacemaking way. Look, I just—"

She didn't return the smile. She just pointed at the door; Uncle Sam wants you—to leave.

I left.

And this time the guy behind the counter didn't smile at me, either.

4

A WARM BREEZE RIFFLED THE FOLIAGE, SUN hiding under some clouds, as I strolled down the plaza of planters and railroad-tie benches and boutiques and trendy cafes, and on the lefthand corner, just as I reached what had once been the intersection where that modern-art sculpture remained stalled, I came to a massive new brown-brick office building, Plaza Centre One. One of its street level shops was filled with yellow and gold merchandise hawking the Hawks, shirts and shoes and caps, usually featuring the U. of Iowa's cartoon mascot, Herky; back in Ginnie's day interest in sports was at its low ebb around here—"Hell no, we won't go!" was one of many battle cries. Now it was, "How 'bout them Hawks!" A copy center and a travel agency flanked the doors as I went in the Centre (which I supposed was much the same as a center), into a stark, modern lobby where silver cylindrical light fixtures hovered like futuristic upside-down ashtrays stuck to the ceiling. I stood studying the building directory, thinking absently that I'd never before been in a high-class office building that smelled quite like this one. As I stood waiting at the bright red elevators, I saw why: tucked back in the corner of this high-tech lobby was the wide counter of a Hardee's Hamburger fast-food outlet, at the moment dispensing early lunch to an odd mix of students and businessmen. This seemed to me a better symbol of Iowa City than Herky the Hawk.

On the fifth floor, I found Multi-Media Consultants, Inc. It was at the end of the hall, glassed in, with a small reception area and a small receptionist. The reception area was mainly smooth yellow walls displaying various awards, framed advertisements, and a few framed original storyboards, with some burlap and pine furniture that had come from ETC.'s, I would guess; a window looked out on the plant-happy plaza. The receptionist had frosted pixie-cut hair, just a little too much makeup and a couple of the sweetest green eyes you even saw in a tan, almost pretty face; she wore a white blouse with pearls of the sort Beaver Cleaver's mother used to wear. She was in her mid-thirties, about my age, and smiled at Sgt. Bilko. We were TV generation, all right.

"You must be a friend of Dave's," she said. Her voice was even deeper than Caroline Westin's, but much more pleasant. She undoubtedly gave good phone; with those nails, she hadn't been hired to type.

I smiled. "You figured out I'm probably not a client."

"Not unless you're one of the eccentric ones." One hand—loaded down with rings, rings loaded down with stones, though none seemed of the wedding variety—curled over the push buttons along the bottom of her phone, long, burnt-orange nails clicking against plastic as she paused before making her interoffice call. "Who shall I say it is?"

"Just say it's a friend of Ginnie Mullens."

Her tanned, wholesome face turned somber. "That was a shame. I liked Ginnie."

"Me too. Did you know her well?"

"Pretty well. Can't I give Mr. Flater your name?"

"Sure. Tell him it's Mallory."

She pointed me down a hallway with a few offices and conference rooms on either side; I walked across a work area where a couple of graphic artists were toiling in cubicles. Flater's door said DAVID F. FLATER and was shut. I knocked and a deep voice said: "Come in."

Flater was a thin man with thinning brown hair and an angular face made more angular by a neatly trimmed spade-shaped beard, designed to hide pockmarks. Not a handsome man, certainly; but not homely. Nine out of ten women would've found his looks "interesting," and the other one, well, who needed her, when you had the other nine?

The room smelled of pot, and a joint smouldered in the ashtray before him. A pair of designer, goggle-type glasses also lay on the desk where they'd been tossed. He was wearing a yellow shirt with no tie, open two buttons at the throat; hair from his chest curled up. A tan sports jacket with patched sleeves lay across a two-drawer file cabinet near the door. There was an untidy bookcase, piled mostly with magazines—*Advertising Age, Adweek*—but a few books—*Confessions of an Advertising Man, From the Wonderful Folks Who Brought You Pearl Harbor,* a demographics study or two—and some video tapes in black plastic boxes.

He didn't rise, but forced a half-smile, waved toward a director's chair opposite his big, modern oak desk.

I sat, glancing around. Behind me was a gallery of pictures, all in black, square, conservative frames: a younger, more fully bearded, less conventionally dressed Flater was shown smiling with the smiling faces of Jerry Rubin, Abbie Hoffmann, Timothy Leary, William Kunstler, Eugene McCarthy. Taken at outdoor rallies, banners with blurred slogans in the background.

"You don't know me," I said, a little nervously, "but . . ."

"You sound like an American Express commercial," he said. Without expression. "Anyway, keep your ID in your pocket. I know you."

"We haven't met."

"Ginnie mentioned you."

"She mentioned *you* to me, when I saw her last."

He sat up a little; spark of interest. "When was that?"

"Our high school reunion last month."

He chuckled, without much humor. His eyes were very red, and I didn't think it was entirely from the pot. "High school reunion. That was the first sign."

"Pardon?"

"That she was getting in one of her reflective moods again. Her existential angst trips again. Jesus!" He lifted the joint like a sacrament and toked it. "I knew I was in trouble any time she brought your goddamn name up."

"Really. Why?"

"Maybe you can tell *me*. I just knew when she did, she'd start talking about the absurdity of life. I'd get quoted everything from *Catch-22* to Samuel Beckett."

Under the stars with Ginnie.

I said, "We used to talk about that sort of thing, back in high school."

"Precocious, weren't you?"

"Why the bitterness?"

"It's not aimed at you."

"Ginnie, then."

He started to take another toke, then pushed it angrily away. "I never did this in my office before."

"What?"

He nodded to the joint in the ashtray, little hairs of smoke rising upward. "I hardly ever use that shit anymore. I just grew out of it."

"Did Ginnie?"

He looked at me sharply, then softened. "Pretty much. I'm not saying recreational drugs were completely a thing of the past, for either of us, but ..."

"Maybe you just outgrew grass."

He laughed; there was some dry humor in it this time. "You sound like Jack Webb. Sure, Mallory—maryjane led me to the hard stuff; I'm shooting skag now. What do you think?"

"I think a guy who uses the term skag at least knows what he's talking about."

He pressed the joint out in the ashtray, dumped it in his wastebasket. "Let's change the subject. What are you doing here, anyway?"

"You and Ginnie had been seeing a lot of each other, the last six months or so."

"That's right. I even lived out at that farmhouse with her, till about a month ago."

"That would've been about the time of our high school reunion."

"Yes, it would. We fought, the next day, as a matter of fact. But it had been brewing."

"You say, you fought?"

He brushed a hand at the air. "Fought.

Argued. Bickered with the amp on ten, get my drift?"

"You just don't look like the hothead type to me, Flater. Even if you *are* ex-SDS."

He leaned forward, smiling in an appraising sort of way, folded his hands. "I do have a certain background in ... protest, not all of it nonviolent."

"Did you grow out of that, too?"

He sighed; his hands still folded, as if in prayer, he glanced out the window at the plaza—the sun was out now, and it danced on the green. "I guess I did. And no one seems to be taking up the mantle, either, do they?" He looked at me, sharply. "Tell me, Mallory—if you were ten, fifteen years younger, wouldn't you take to the streets again? Wouldn't you have something to carry a placard about? The threat of nuclear annihilation, maybe? A warmongering White House? Pollution? *Something?*"

"I don't know. Maybe."

"You were a protestor. Ginnie told me."

"I was involved in a veterans-against-the-war group. We lobbied, we didn't riot. We worked within the system."

"Oh, isn't that sweet! A condescending tone for those of us who really got out and got it done."

"I didn't mean to be condescending. People like you helped stop the war; I won't take that away from you."

He laughed from down in his chest; I never heard a laugh more bitter. "Isn't that *big* of you. Where are you, now? What are you doing now, for the cause?"

"What cause?"

That threw him for a minute.

Then he said, "Any cause. Any good human cause."

"I write mysteries. You write ads. So spare me the condescension, too, while you're at it."

With tight, barely restrained anger, he said, "My agency has handled the campaigns for a dozen Democratic candidates on state and national levels, for *cost*."

"You're doing a hell of a job, too, judging by all the Republicans getting elected."

Looking out the window again, he said, "We do what we can."

"Wasn't there some bad publicity that probably helped lose an election for that guy, what's-his-name, who was running for U.S. Senate a while back? When it came out his ad campaign was being run by the former Propaganda Minister of the Yippies?"

He just nodded, as if he barely remembered I was there.

I said, "I doubt any politicians will be using your agency again, even if you do give your services to 'em at cost."

Still looking out the window, he smiled faintly. "I have other clients, including some rather conservative ones, who are able to coexist peacefully with the radical skeletons in my closet. I have three national TV spots airing this month, Mallory. And I have the single largest advertising account in the state; don't let my modest offices fool you."

I hadn't found his offices particularly modest—or him, either, for that matter.

I said, "I suppose you're talking about Life-Investors Mutual."

One of the hundred top insurance companies in the world.

"That's right," he said.

"Ain't it great," I said.

He looked at me. "What?"

"Capitalism."

He gave me a smile that was almost a sneer and said, "I never, ever said I was anything but a capitalist. I also happen to be a socialist, and those terms aren't contradictory."

"Whatever you say."

"You are a shallow son of a bitch, Mallory. I wonder what Ginnie saw in you."

"You took the words right out of my mouth."

He opened a drawer and took out a pipe; not the hashish variety, either. He poked some tobacco in and lit up. "Did you ever make it with Ginnie?" he asked.

"No. We were never that way."

"Just friends."

"That's right."

"Are you gay or something?"

"I'm gay in the sense that I'm a cheerful sort of guy. Other than that, how would you like to ride that pipe?"

He patted the air with his free hand,

drawing on the pipe like an older, wiser man than I would ever be. "Take it easy. I just wondered. Ginnie was . . . well, you know how she was. She seemed to be open, telling you the damnedest things, to shock, to provoke, to entertain you. But she kept certain things to herself. And despite her mentioning you frequently . . . well, not frequently, but enough that it got on my nerves . . . I never got a sense of what your relationship might've been like."

"We were friends," I said. "We grew up together."

"Brother and sister sort of thing."

"If you insist. I think of it as friendship and let it go at that."

"I, uh . . . guess we're both a little testy. We've both suffered a loss."

"Yes we have."

"I loved Ginnie, you know."

"I did, too, in my way. Do you mind my asking a personal question?"

"Ask, and we'll see."

"Why did you and Ginnie break it off?"

He leaned back in his chair, thinking, puffing. The pipe smoke was overly sweet smelling and mingled with the pot smell in a way that turned my stomach.

He said, "I tried to honor her . . . independence. We had an open sort of relationship. We could see other people, if we liked. And sometimes we did. That . . . that didn't bother me. At times I even liked it; my profession is one . . . conducive to promiscuity."

An ad man ought to be able to come up with a better way to say "screwing around" than that. But I didn't point it out.

He went on. "It was certain other habits of hers that I couldn't put up with."

"Such as?"

He sighed again. "She's barely gone. Do we have to talk about that side of her?"

"What side? Was she doing drugs?"

"Drugs wasn't the problem. Not really."

"What was?"

He winced. "She was too wild."

"Wild. Not sexually . . ."

"No! Well, that, too. But that I could live with. It was a, well . . ."

"Trade-off. It let you tomcat around if you felt like it."

He smiled, barely. " 'Tomcat.' That's a term I haven't heard in a while. You really are a small-town boy, aren't you?"

"I meant to say, it allowed you to lead a life more conducive to promiscuity."

"Okay. So I called you a hick, and you called me a pompous ass. Can we move on?"

"Sure. Move on to why you and Ginnie really broke up."

"I couldn't handle her. Couldn't handle it."

"What?"

He put on his glasses; they were tinted, obscuring his eyes. "Well," he said, sitting back. "You might say I'd about had it with that angst in her pants routine. Long all-night bull sessions about the meaning of life with somebody who hadn't really grown up yet after thirty-some years on this planet, immature crap, as far as I was concerned, considering what she was doing with her life."

"What *was* she doing with her life? What *was* bothering you about her?"

"Frankly—the gambling. It wasn't just that she lost money. After all, sometimes she'd win. But it was just too much. She would have a lunch appointment with me, and wouldn't show up. I'd go home that night and find a note saying, 'Gone to Vegas.' Or Tahoe, or even Atlantic City."

"She'd just go at the drop of a hat."

He nodded. "Yes. And the drop of thousands of dollars."

"Was she losing?"

He shrugged. "She had her ups and downs."

"What about lately?"

"Downs. I'd say, downs."

I had a hunch; I played it.

I said, "Before you broke up, had she made a Vegas trip recently?"

"Tahoe, actually."

"Did she use her own money?"

He thought about that before answering. Reluctantly, against his better judgment, he revealed, "She took ten thousand dollars of mine."

"Where'd she get her hands on that much cash?"

"We had a joint account. It was something

she'd been trying to talk me into for a while. As a show of confidence."

"And you showed her confidence, and she conned you."

"Essentially, yes."

"Did she pay you back?"

"No. She said she would, though."

"What do you know about her selling ETC.'s?"

"Not much. I think she may have played the same sort of game with Caroline as me, though. Caroline Westin is not the sort who'd put up with that kind of thing very long."

"Why'd Ginnie take your ten grand? She must've had money left from the sale of ETC.'s."

"She got a hundred grand on that deal. But the money hadn't come through yet, when she took that Tahoe fling."

"Had it come through before yesterday?"

"I believe so."

"But she made no move to pay you back?"

"No."

"Do you think she would've?"

"I'm not sure. We broke off pretty bitterly."

"How did you feel about her, after you broke it off?"

"I hated her. And I loved her. Haven't you ever known any women, Mallory?"

I stood. "Yeah. A couple. Thanks for the conversation, Flater."

He stood; he thought about it, then offered

his hand. "I suppose there's no reason for us to be assholes to each other."

I thought about it, agreed, shook his hand.

He came out from around his desk, slipped on his patched sports coat, checking his watch. "I have an early luncheon appointment. I'll walk out with you."

We walked silently out into the reception area, where he said to the receptionist, "I'll be back by two-thirty, Shirley."

A burnt-orange nail pointing to the appointment book open on her desk, Shirley said, "Don't forget your three-thirty appointment in Cedar Rapids, at Investors Mutual."

"I guess I *won't* be back at two-thirty," he said, to her, smiling a little. "See you tomorrow."

Shirley smiled at him, then at me, and Flater and I stepped out into the hall, walked to the elevators.

He said, "Do you know when the funeral is?"

"Tomorrow morning. Graveside services at Greenwood Cemetery in Port City."

"I'll be there."

The red elevator doors slid open, and as he got on, I said, "I think I forgot something back there. See you tomorrow."

He nodded, and the doors slid shut.

I stood looking at the red doors, thinking about the former Yippie propaganda minister who couldn't abide Ginnie's me-generation searching, her reckless life style. And, while the irony was hardly lost on me, I couldn't blame him.

Then I went back and asked Shirley what she was doing after work.

5

IT WAS TURNING INTO ONE OF THOSE SUMMER days that convinced you Iowa City was half trees, half parking lots: almost noon, now—here the sun careened off cement, there it shimmied down through leaves, catching your eyes in a crossfire. I had sunglasses on, but you could've fooled me. Sun also bounced off the police station, which was part of the Civic Center (or was that Centre?), a sprawl of tan brick and tinted glass on the edge of the downtown, on the corner of Washington and Van Buren to be exact, where university buildings and small businesses began giving way to residences and frat houses.

Like most public buildings in Iowa City, this one looked like a school, specifically a split-level schoolhouse circa 1957, with a vaguely Spanish look, partially due to the cement lattice work the building hid behind, partially due to California-style trees and shrubs surrounding the place like Indians around a wagon train.

A dark lanky guy in mirrored sunglasses, a long-sleeved white shirt (rolled up at the elbows), new jeans (held up by a turquoise-and-silver-buckled belt), cowboy boots (detailed leather) and a Zapata mustache (trimmed neatly) rolled out of the building via the revolving door in front. I was sitting on a bench not unlike the ones in the plaza outside Flater's office; this place may have been a plice station, but what it wanted to be was Knotts Berry Farm.

"You'd be Mallory," the lanky guy said.

I stood. "You're Evans."

"Yeah," he said. "My friends call me Ev."

I smiled at the wry uncertainty in his voice. "But I can call you Detective Evans?"

He grinned; he had a big white dazzler of a grin that seemed faintly familiar to me, though I'd never seen him before. He looked like a Mexican outlaw with that tan, lined face; but he was a midwest mutt like me, mixed Irish and English and what-have-you, and about my age. He looked ten years older than me, easy, and I look my age.

"Well," he said, "you said look for a guy in a Sgt. Bilko T-shirt. And you seem to be the only one of those around."

"Beats wearing a red carnation," I said. I

was standing now, and we seemed to be walking up toward the business district.

"I checked with Brennan," he said, "after you called this morning. He said I should help you out any way I can."

"That'd be great, if you would."

"Why not? Brennan's good people."

Detective Evans wasn't wearing a gun on his hip, but he did have a square black object in one shirt pocket: a beeper, I supposed.

"How 'bout I buy you lunch at Bushnell's?" I proposed.

"How 'bout you do that? And I'll do my best to answer your questions."

Bushnell's Turtle was a restaurant just across from Flater's Centre in the plaza, a two-story brick building trimmed in green and yellow, dating to 1883, painstakingly restored. The interior was fairly intimate, pastel green walls alternating with salmon ones, lots of classy old oak woodwork, the occasional stain-glass window and the more than occasional standing plant. Keeping our sunglasses on, Evans and I read aloud from the green chalkboard menu while a kid in jeans wrote our orders down, handing us our tickets which we took to a massive oak and marble counter, a bar actually, paying at an ancient cash register while our orders were filled.

It was pretty crowded—kids in shorts and backpacks predominated—but not like it would've been during the school year. We carried trays with our food to a booth, ate our soup (navy bean, delicious) and began talking and eating our submarine sandwiches. A man named Bushnell invented the Submarine, incidentally. The ship, not the sandwich.

"I notice you don't carry a gun," I said.

"Sometimes I do," he said, nibbling at his sub (sandwich, not ship). "But not when I eat at a hippie joint like this."

That seemed a quaint, if relatively accurate, way to put it.

I said, "*Is* there such a thing as a hippie around these parts anymore? I thought it was a dead species."

He continued nibbling the sandwich; he was a strangely dainty eater. "Some of these kids are still that way. And there's burnt-outs from the old days, still hangin' around, and professional students, and teachers that are just yesterday's hippies retread."

"I see short hair and beer, everywhere I look. Not long hair and pot."

"Oh, there's dope bein' smoked. And so on."

"Not as much as there used to be."

"Not among the kids, maybe."

"By which you mean . . . ?"

For the first time since we got there, his attention went from his sandwich to me; the mirrors of his sunglasses showed me in my sunglasses looking back at myself. "It's the grown-ups, bud. The old hippies. The ones that run the businesses. That run for office. That teach the classes. The Commies in designer undies."

The latter was said with a certain wry humor; Evans was no redneck—or, if he was, it was by choice.

I asked him where he grew up.

"Around here," he said, returning his attention to his sandwich. "Nichols, actually."

That was a small farm community just twenty miles from Iowa City.

I said, "Did you go to school here at the University?"

"No. I got a four-year law enforcement degree through Port City Community, though."

"That's where I went."

"No kiddin'? When?"

"Mid-seventies."

"I was just before you, then. Nam? G.I. Bill?"

"Yeah."

He smiled; it was as wide as the grill of a Cadillac. He took off the mirrored shades. His eyes were sky blue. "Me too."

I took off my sunglasses. "Here's looking at you," I said, hoisting my ginger ale.

"So that's the connection," he said, smiling smaller now, thinking like a detective. "You'd've been a buddy of Brennan's kid. Uh, Jack?"

"John. His name was John."

He sobered. "Bought the farm, I hear."

"Yeah. The whole damn plantation."

"I never knew him. Good guy?"

"The best. We enlisted together."

"Were you . . . ?"

He trailed off, but I knew the question. Any vet would've.

I said, "No, I wasn't with him. I was wounded and went home, before it happened. He stayed in. He didn't buy it till the bitter fucking end. The evacuation, in '75. He was flying Air America."

Evans almost shuddered. "I didn't have the *cojones* for that mercenary shit. Duty that heavy I never did need."

"John liked the military. I think he liked the action, too."

"I can understand that. Being in law enforcement is that way, in a way. But Vietnam, that was one hell-hole. I was glad to get free of it."

"Me too."

He laughed. "Funny thing is, we bust our butts, and the hippies inherit the earth."

"How do you mean?"

He kept his voice down, leaning forward, half a sub in one hand like a weapon he was keeping handy. "They own everything around here. Look around this downtown. It looks like Disneyland if Joan Baez invented it."

I laughed at that. "That's a good line. I may use it."

"Oh yeah. Brennan said you're a writer. What do you write?"

"Mysteries."

"Name a couple."

I did.

He said, "Haven't read 'em." Looking for a way to connect, he said, "I like the Executioner, though. I read all of those."

"What can you tell me about Ginnie Mullens?"

He chewed a bite of his sandwich; began talking before he swallowed it. "She's a good example of what I was talking about before. She was a campus radical. SDS. Yippie. The whole route. Ran a head shop. Look what it turned into."

"It's turned into a nice little business."

"Yeah, there's been mucho dough made there, over the years." He leaned forward again. "Not all of it from furniture and imported coffee, either."

"What do you mean?"

He snuffled with his nose in an exaggerated manner several times.

"Cocaine," I said, very softly.

"And every mother-lovin' thing else in that line of product, over the years."

"Ginnie was a dealer."

"From word go. From when she first opened that little hole-in-the-wall shop on Dubuque."

"Did your departmet try to do anything about it?"

He shrugged. "We warned her from time to time. Tell you the truth, this all began before I was on the force. Hell, it began when I was still playing rice-paddy polo. She opened the first version of ETC.'s around '70, '71."

"Strictly a head shop."

"No—she always had the apartment-store angle; that was her cover. She'd go down to Mexico to buy jewelry and art pieces and furniture and such, to sell in the shop."

"And while she was in Mexico, she'd also pick up certain other goods."

"Exactly."

"She was never busted."

"I don't think so. Not by the border cops, or us, either."

"How do you explain that?"

"The border cops, I couldn't say. As for around these parts, well. There's been a lot of benign neglect in certain areas, where the department's concerned. In a college town like this, you can't be too big a rightwing hardass. Knee-jerk liberals run things around here, and the locals who don't fall in that category, the sort who are born and live and die here, know enough not to make waves. My understanding—and this is just my opinion, now, not official in the leastways—is that during the seventies and maybe beyond, as long as the likes of Ginnie Mullens didn't get too brazen, kept things nice and low-profile, law enforcement looked the other way."

"There *have* been drug busts up here."

"Sure. If we see it, we do something about it. If we see it."

"But you don't go looking for it."

He Shrugged again. "When in Rome."

"Did local law enforcement look the other way where Ginnie Mullens's dealing was concerned?"

"Yes and no. She was supposedly dealing locally up to five years ago."

"Then what happened?"

"She got sloppy. And cocky. Bad combination. Started talking freely about what she was up to. Right in her store, right in the middle of it expanding into what it's become, a major damn business in its own right, she's dealing on the premises, talking right out in the open about ludes, coke, pills, what have you, dealing on the *premises*, for Christ's sake."

"You said she was never busted?"

"She was warned. She was strongly advised to stop dealing."

"Who by?"

"Never mind that. Not by me, I'm a little fish. I only been a detective three years now. And if I get too loose at the mouth with you, bud, I'll be back directing traffic outside of Carver Hawkeye Arena after basketball games, get my drift?"

"Did she stop dealing?"

"I heard she did. My understanding—this is not gospel, this is rumor, okay? My understanding is the Chamber of Commerce—she was a member—was nervous about the way she was conducting herself and asked somebody at the department to scare her a little. Scare her into cleaning up her act."

"But *did* she?"

"I don't know. I hear yes, but I don't really know. I never met the lady. I saw her around, but I never spoke to her in my life."

Soon we were walking back toward the Civic Center. A new Holiday Inn loomed at our right, cutting across the plaza at an angle, a tan, modern building with lots of windows and along the side a restaurant with pregnant greenhouse windows. Iowa City so desperately wanted to be California, in the midst of a cornfield.

"What I don't understand about Ginnie Mullens," Evans said, loping along, "is why she bothered dealing at all. With a straight, successful business the likes of ETC.'s, it don't make sense."

"Maybe she had a habit to support," I said.

He grunted, and made the exaggerated snuffling sound again.

"Not that kind of habit," I said.

"Then, what?"

"She gambled."

"No kidding. Vegas type of thing, you mean?"

"Yeah."

"I never heard that."

"No reason you should have. But if she was dealing drugs, it was to feed her gambling habit. At least that probably was part of it."

We were back at the Civic Center.

Evans said, "What else?"

I shrugged. "She liked gambling in more ways than just the Las Vegas sense. She was a risk taker."

"I guess I can dig it," he said. The phrase seemed odd, coming from him, and at the same time exactly right. "Like your buddy John. Like all our crazy-ass friends who re-upped when they shoulda hung it up.

Gone home and found some nice safe civilian gig."

I smiled. "Like being a cop?"

He smiled; his smile again reminded me of someone else's. Who did I know that had a great big dazzling grin like that?

Oh.

John.

"Look," he said, "I don't know exactly what you're up to here, asking around about the Mullens gal. But I can give you a name that might get you somewhere. Only the somewhere it gets you could be up shit crick."

"How so?"

He leaned forward, glanced around both ways before he spoke. What was this, a spy movie?

He said, "There's a guy in town who's a major connection. I don't just mean Iowa City."

"Yeah? What's his name?"

"Sturms. Marlon H."

"Got an address?"

"Try the phone book," he said. "That's what us detectives do."

Then, with a little wave and one more big smile, he turned, walked up to the schoolhouse Civic Center, and went back in the revolving door.

6

ON THE EDGE OF IOWA CITY, ON ONE OF THE less traveled routes out of town, on a street called Port City Avenue, I paused at a sign that had a red circle with a slash through the word Noise. Below the red circle and slash it said: Noise Ordinance Strictly Enforced. Who you gonna call? Noisebusters. I turned right into an expensive housing development sprawled over gently rolling hills. In these split-level palaces professionals dwelled. Doctors. Lawyers. The occasional well-tenured professor.

And a drug dealer. Not the prescription variety, either, as found in nearby Towncrest medical center, where some of these professionals worked. Rather, a dealer in illegal, under-the-counter, recreational-type chemical substances. And to live in this neck of the woods with the Towncrest crowd, this dealer in such substances would have to be, as Detective Evans had said, "a major connection." And a half.

And, as Detective Evans had said, Marlon H. Sturms was in the phone book. So was the Sturms, Marlon H. Insurance Company of Iowa City, but when I called that number, I got an answering service. Mr. Sturms was not in his office. Maybe he was home. I didn't call to find out—I just dropped by.

The house was one of the few nonsplit-levels in the neighborhood, though it had the same sloping spacious lawn as its neighbors. This modest cottage was a barn out of Frank Lloyd Wright, three stories of dark, stained, "natural" wood, the color varying from rust to a dirty brown, with windows that gave it the face of a jack-o'-lantern. None of the windows was shaded, but sun bounced off them and made them opaque. There was a one-story, two-car garage off to the right, a red Mercedes parked in the drive; I pulled my silver Firebird in alongside it. There were some antique metal farm implements arranged in the front yard, like a modern sculpture that wasn't abstract enough. The sidewalk and the rough redwood fence that followed it took four fashionable jogs up to the front door. So did I.

The doorbell played a tune, but I didn't recognize it. Someone in the house apparently did, because soon the door cracked open. There was a nightlatch. A cautious eye peeked out, in a sliver of what seemed to be tan female face.

"Oh, good!" The voice attached to the face was also female; and if a voice could be tan, this was it.

She opened the door wide and smiled at me. "I didn't think you could make it today."

She was rather tall, trim but shapely, with medium-length, Annie-permed auburn hair, striking large brown eyes and occasional streaks of color on her face. It wasn't makeup. It was also on her short-sleeve gray sweatshirt and on her white jogging shorts, blue, gray, yellow, brown, slashes and dabs. Paint.

I said "Pardon me, I . . ."

"Come in, come in."

I shrugged and stepped inside. The living room went as high as the roof, with the second and third floors only half as wide as the house, their balconies looking at me from across the room. The walls inside were barnwood as well, but the furnishings were cool and modern and costly, everything appointed in white and beige and other almost-colors. The only splashes of real color were provided by a dozen meaningless paintings, spatterings of color on canvas. All obviously by the same artist—compared to whom Jackson Pollock was a realist.

"You'll have to excuse me," she said, gesturing to her paint-streaky self. "I'm in the middle of a canvas."

I had a sudden image of her creating her

masterworks by stepping on tubes of paint that had been scattered across a prone canvas. Like stomping grapes to make wine. Or, in this case, grape Kool-aid.

But that obviously wasn't her work method. In the middle of the living room floor a dropcloth spread like a rumpled stain; in its midst was a canvas on an easel. A work in progress. Yellow attacking a field of blue.

"You're an artist," I said.

"Yes," she beamed, then turned. She was heading across the room.

I was still just inside the door. I said, "Excuse me."

She stopped, looked back over her shoulder at me. Her jogging shorts had a few streaks of paint across them; the most attractive canvas in the house.

"It's in here," she said, pointing to a hallway below the second-floor overhang.

"What?"

She turned and looked at me with puzzlement and a little annoyance. "The softener!"

"Who do you think I am?"

"The Culligan man!"

I opened the door to leave, smiling, shaking my head. "I'm sorry to disappoint you. I'm not here to service your water softener."

She looked me over, in my Bilko T-shirt and camouflage shorts, and said, "Then what are you doing in my house?"

There was no fear in it, or anger; it was just a question.

"I'm looking for Marlon Sturms. This *is* his home, isn't it?"

"And mine," she said; she didn't cross to me—kept the room between us. "I'm Mrs. Sturms."

"Pleased to meet you. My name is Mallory."

"Is my husband expecting you?"

"Is he here?"

"Yes."

Maybe he was, maybe he wasn't; if I was in her shoes, having accidentally admitted a strange man to my house, I'd say he was home.

"He doesn't know me," I said, "but we had a mutual friend. Ginnie Mullens."

"Oh, yes," she said. Softening. She leaned against a white lounge chair, apparently not worried about getting paint on it. "She died, didn't she? It was on the radio. 'Gunshot wound, possibly self-inflicted.' That's sad."

"Yes it is."

"I knew Ginnie, but not very well."

"Really."

"Marlon thought highly of her. He was upset this morning, when we heard about it."

"I'd like to talk to him about her."

"Well . . ."

"Please?"

"Why don't you step outside, and I'll see."

"Sure," I said.

I stepped out on the porch.

A few minutes later she cracked the door open. The latch was in place again.

She said, "Marlon isn't here, but I called the club. You know where the country club is? Across the river and up the hill?"

"Yes," I said, resisting the impulse to add, "To Grandmother's house we go."

"You can meet him in the club lounge, in about an hour."

"Fine. Thank you. How will I know him?"

"I told him what you're wearing. He'll find you."

And he did. I'd been sitting at the bar on a high-backed stool in the small, not-very-busy lounge, working on a bottle of Pabst, for less than three minutes when he approached me. He looked tan, his lime polo shirt sticking to him a little after his eighteen holes, and very much over the shock of Ginnie Mullens dying.

He extended a hand and his grip was firm but disinterested. He had a crooked smile and a flat, broad nose in an otherwise handsome face, his hair short, brown, and styled, his build trimly muscular. He looked like the kind of man who reads *Playboy*.

I told him my name as we shook hands.

"I know who you are," he said, sitting. His voice was tenor, and a little bored. Jaded. He nodded to the bartender, who knew what to bring him based upon the gesture.

"How do you know me?" I said. "I don't remember that we ever met."

"We haven't."

The bartender deposited a martini before him. The eye of its olive looked at me; Sturms didn't.

"If we haven't met, then . . . ?"

He smiled at me with bland condescension. "You're a mystery writer. I saw that article about you in the Des Moines *Register.*"

"Why should you remember me from that?"

"I don't. I know you from Ginnie. She used to mention you."

"You were a friend of Ginnie's."

"We were friendly."

"You don't seem too broken up about her death."

"How I feel about her death is my business. Why did you want to see me, Mallory?"

"I'm trying to put the pieces together. I want to know what happened to Ginnie, and why."

"Researching another book?"

"No."

He raised his martini, looked into it like a crystal ball. The olive eye looked back at him. Neither one of them gave a damn.

"Might be a book in it for you," he said with empty cheer. Then, with mock pomp, went on: "*Whatever Happened to the Love Generation?* You could compare the dreams and the platitudes of the sixties flower children with the disappointing realities and hypocrisies of their lives in the seventies and eighties. Ginnie might make a good symbol of that."

"So would you."

Without looking at me, he smiled, still contemplating the drink. "I was never a flower child."

"Or a doper?"

"Or a doper."

"No, I guess not," I said. "I'll bet you were a frat rat, in those days, weren't you? Sigma something."

He saluted me with his glass. "It's Greek to me," he said.

"You were never vaguely a hippie. You've been a capitalist all along."

He turned in his seat, smiling. There was more warmth in the olive than in his smile. He said, "My father left me an insurance business. He was a bad businessman—a nice fella, but a bad businessman. I've made his business thrive. I'm a respected member of the community, Mallory. A member here at the club. A property owner. Whatever could you be implying?"

"Do you want me to say it?"

The lounge was almost empty, and the bartender was at the other end of the bar. Still, it was a public place.

Very softly, he said, "You think I'm a dealer. Let's suppose you're right. Let's suppose I do have a ... sideline. And let's suppose further that Ginnie was in the same business. That we were business partners."

"Let's."

"Fine. But Ginnie and I weren't partners anymore. We stayed friends. I saw her from time to time. Strictly got together to ... how did they put it in the sixties?" With heavy sarcasm, he said, "We'd ... *rap*."

"I bet you majored in business."

"That's right, and all the sixties meant to me was business. Oh, yeah, and a few days of no classes after Kent State."

"You started dealing back then, I'll bet. Just helping out friends, and friends of friends. And like any good business, it grew."

His boredom was turning to irritation. "Is there anything else? I'd like to get home to my wife."

"Beautiful woman. She was working on a painting."

"Keeps her off the streets."

"Five years ago the local law told Ginnie to quit dealing. Told her it wasn't respectable for somebody running a place like ETC.'s."

He nodded. "And she did what they told her."

"Are you sure of that?"

"Sure I'm sure. She quit dealing. She was doing fine with her shop; who needed it?"

"She had a gambling habit, you know."

He laughed, a scoffing sort of laugh. "So she went to Vegas and Tahoe when she needed to cut loose. So what? Gambling habit, ha."

The bartender came around and picked up Sturms's empty glass; he didn't order another.

"Now," he said, "I've done you the courtesy of meeting with you. Now why don't you do me the courtesy of leaving? Members and their guests only here—I'm about to go down and take a shower before I go home. And you're about to be nobody's guest."

7

WE SAT AMIDST PLANTS OF ALL PERSUASIONS in a little bar/deli named after Amelia Earhart. I was having another Pabst, and she was having a Coors Light. Her eyes were greener thin the plants.

"So you're a writer?" she said, smiling nervously, her free hand tugging at the June Cleaver pearls.

"That's right, Shirl."

We had already decided that she would be Shirl, and I would be Mal.

"Not a copywriter, though," she said.

"No—I wasn't up to see your boss about an ad-writing job. Like I told you, we were both friends of Ginnie Mullens and I wanted to do some mutual commiserating."

She shrugged with her eyes. "Dave was

pretty miserable about it. They broke up, but he's still carrying the torch."

"I notice you refer to him as Dave, not Mr. Flater."

She shrugged with her shoulders. "Don't read anything into that. Dave just runs a casual shop. He likes his clients to feel among friends, and he makes his employees feel the same way."

"You aren't dating him or anything."

"I've seen him socially a few times. What kind of writer are you, if you aren't a copywriter?"

"Novelist."

She brightened. "Really? What have you written?"

"I write mysteries." I mentioned the name of the latest one.

She dimmed. "I don't read mysteries, sorry. I'm afraid I'm one of those women into historical romances."

"They make terrific escape, and some of 'em are very nicely written. When was the last time Dave saw Ginnie?"

"As far as I know, it was almost a month ago. It really broke off sudden."

"Is that something you just gathered, or . . . ?"

"I heard it. The tail end of it, anyway. She came up to Multi-Media and they went in his office and you could hear them arguing clear out at my reception desk. I never heard them argue like that before. They used to kid on the square sometimes, your normal good-natured sniping. Only this time they really blew, and she came storming out."

"Did you hear her say anything to him?"

She made an embarrassed face. "Yeah."

"What?"

She leaned forward and whispered: "She said, 'You'll get your goddamn money, asshole,' and, boom, went out the door."

"Did Flater follow her?"

"No. He just stood there with a real red face."

"Then what?"

A different sort of embarrassment. "Then he asked me out to dinner."

"I see."

"No, you don't. We'd seen each other a few times, while he and Ginnie were thick. They had your basic open relationship ... and, well, hey—I found Dave attractive, and he's my boss, and I liked Ginnie okay, but I went out with him a few times, anyway, 'cause he asked. And I admit it made me uncomfortable, after, and I asked him to cool it, at least as long as he and Ginnie were an item."

"So when Ginnie stormed out, and he asked you to dinner, it was ..."

"It was punctuation at the end of a sentence, if you know what I mean. It was like he was saying it for her benefit, even though she wasn't around. Weird, but true."

"But you haven't dated him much since."

"That was the last time. We didn't have much fun. He was very blue about breaking up with Ginnie, blue and ... angry, I guess.

I've had that kind of relationship, haven't you?"

"What kind?"

She sighed. "Where you bust up with somebody over something they said or did, and then you get to feeling blue, thinking about how much you miss them and how you wish you could patch things up with them, but when you start thinking about why you busted up exactly, you get mad all over again."

"Yeah. I've had that kind of relationship."

She grinned. "Who hasn't? Say, why are you asking all these questions about Ginnie, and Dave?"

I poured the last of my Pabst bottle into my glass. "It's not Dave, really. It's Ginnie I'm interested in. I went to high school with her, and we were close. Drifted apart. Now she's dead, and I'm trying to make some sense of it."

She gave me a puzzled look; boy, her eyes were green. "That's a funny sort of thing to do."

"Is it?"

"It's not unusual to mope around thinking about somebody after they die, and try and make sense out of it. But to go around asking people questions, like in *Citizen Kane* or something, that's odd."

I smiled a little. "You like old movies?"

She smiled a little back at me. "Sure."

"Want to take one in some time, at the Bijou?"

"I go there all the time. Sometimes I take my daughter."

"Oh, so you have a little girl."

"Yeah. Seven years. I'm divorced."

"Most single people our age are."

"Are you?"

"I'm the exception that proves the rule."

"I've never understood that expression. You're a writer—why don't you explain it to me?"

"I've never understood it either. That doesn't stop me from using it, though."

She sipped her glass of Coors. "You're an odd duck. Maybe it's because you're a writer."

"It's because I'm a mystery writer, probably."

"Trying to put puzzles together."

"Yeah. Trying to make things make sense. Trying to make life tidy and neat."

"Which it isn't."

"Which it isn't. But trying, anyway. Do you know a guy named Sturms?"

"Sure," she said, not looking at me. "He's an insurance man."

"Ever hear anything else about him?"

"Such as?"

"Such as, I don't know. Just wondering."

"No. He's Dave's insurance man, that's all I know."

"Really. Does he ever come to see Dave, at the office?"

"Sure. He was in this morning."

Interesting.

"Like another beer, Shirl?"

"No. Thank you. This'll do me." She glanced at a round clock on the pine wall, surrounded by shrubbery. "It's almost five. I have to pick my little girl up at the sitter's in fifteen minutes."

"Thanks for taking off early, so we could have this little chat."

"It's okay. Dave's loose. Anytime after four, I can go if I need to, or just feel like it."

"He sounds like a good boss."

"He really is."

I walked her from Amelia Earhart's around the corner and a couple blocks down, to a parking ramp where her car was. Mine, too, actually.

On the way, I said, "You must be about my age—probably a little younger, though."

"I'm thirty-three."

"You're a year younger than me. Can I ask you a question?"

With nice dry humor, she said, "It's a little bit late to start asking me if you can ask questions, Mal, isn't it?"

I put my arm in hers; she seemed to like it.

"You're right," I said. "But I wanted to get a little personal."

"I've been sort of hoping you would."

"What's your attitude toward drugs? Recreational ones, I mean.

"Well," she said thoughtfully, "I've used some over the years. I may not look it today, prim and proper and all, but I did acid, once upon a time. Among other things."

"And?"

"And I never had a single flashback, and I never sat and stared at the sun till I went blind, either."

"Good for you. So, are you still into that, at all?"

"No. That's kid stuff, don't you think?"

"I do, actually. But a lot of people don't."

"I have a little girl of my own. I don't have any of that stuff in my house. I see it at parties sometimes, but stay away from it, even there."

"Why?"

We were at the parking ramp.

"I wasn't a campus radical or anything," she said. "But I'm the right age to remember what people said back then. What sort of changes they hoped to make. The Woodstock nation, give peace a chance, dawning of the age of Aquarius, all of it. And what became of it all? Look at Dave—he was a mover and shaker in those days, in those circles. And now he sells advertising. Oh, he does a great job at it, I'm all for it. But isn't it funny how the only thing left from those days is the dope? The ideals, they're all gone. But the dope is still here. And what good has ever come from it?"

I didn't have an answer for her.

"Ginnie was part of that," she said suddenly. "I didn't know her but to speak to her, but she was part of that."

"Part of what? Dope?"

"Yes."

"She still used it?"

"Oh, probably. She used to be a dealer, everybody knows that."

"Was she still?"

"I don't know. Maybe not. I'm just an outsider."

"Shirl, if you know something, please tell me."

"I don't, really."

"All right." I let some air out, took her by both her hands, squeezed gently. "Thanks for having a beer with me. I'd like to see you again some time."

"Even though you found out I have a little girl at home?"

I grinned at her. "If I didn't go out with women who have kids at home, I'd have to restrict my dating to preteens. And I'm getting a little long in the tooth for that. I like women my own age."

"Is that why you wear the Sgt. Bilko T-shirt?"

"What do you mean?"

"If a girl recognizes Bilko, then she's old enough to date you, is that it?"

I laughed. "Subconsciously, that could be the reason. Never thought of it that way. Could I have your phone number?"

She got a little piece of paper out of her purse and wrote the number on it and gave it to me.

"Please call," she said. "I like you, Mal."

"I like you too, Shirl. And I bet I'll like your kid, too. It, uh, may be a week or so before you hear from me."

"You're going to be asking around about Ginnie."

"Yes."

"Just 'cause you're curious about what made her tick."

"I'm curious about what made her stop ticking."

"Maybe you shouldn't be."

"Why not?"

"Didn't you listen to me before? I said Ginnie was part of it, Mal."

"Dope."

"Yes, and where there's dope, there's fire."

"That's an interesting way of putting it."

"I didn't want to tell you, but somebody's got to. That man you mentioned. That insurance agent."

"Sturms."

"Him. He's the biggest coke dealer around."

"Is your boss involved with him . . . ?"

"In dope? I don't know, and I don't care. As far as I know, he's just Dave's insurance agent. But I've lived in this town since I was in high school, and Sturms is a fixture. And Ginnie was tight with him."

"That's what I understand. And that strikes me as strange—after all, he's an ex-preppie and Ginnie was an ex-hippie. What do they have to be friends about? Sturms doesn't hit me as Ginnie's cup of tea at all—herbal or otherwise."

"Must not have been friendship, then."

"What else, then?"

"What's left? Business." She walked toward

the ramp, then glanced back at me, green eyes flashing. "I'd like to hear from you, when you get this out of your system."

"You will, Shirl."

When I got this out of my system.

8

THE FUNERAL HOME WAS ON WEST THIRD, in the first block beyond the business district in a stately, pillared old house typical of those on West Hill. West Hill was, after all, where the mansions and near-mansions of Port City's first millionaires and near-millionaires had roosted, looking down on the Mississippi River (and the rest of Port City). More recent generations of the very wealthy had, for the most part, departed West Hill for condominiums and split-levels, usually out of state, and some of the grand gothic dwellings of their forefathers weren't maintained like they should. The home I was parking in front of was an exception, a soft-focus oasis in the night, basking in pastel lighting, looking much better than most of its neighbors, looking just like it had twenty, fifty, a hundred years ago, perfectly preserved, a masterpiece of embalming.

The smell of flowers and a guy in a dark suit met me at the door. He was several years younger than I, but seemed infinitely wiser—his smile, which was barely there, was delivered with practiced compassion. I was no longer wearing the Bilko T-shirt and camouflage shorts (and shame on you for thinking I might be) but hadn't quite seen my way to a suit, wearing a short-sleeve white shirt and gray slacks. The suit could wait for the graveside services tomorrow morning; I was just here for "family visitation." The guy, a sort of maître d' of death, led me by the arm to the guest book, which was on a little table at the foot of stairs that rose to darkness. I wasn't interested in what was upstairs at a funeral parlor. I was even less interested in what was in the cellar.

I signed the guest book—under a flowing signature that spelled out another name from the past: Jill Forest. I'd dated her a few times, years ago. I glanced up the page and got no other similar twinges from yesterday. I did see Brennan's signature.

Visitation rooms, as they say in the trade, were to my right and left. The one at right wasn't being used; the one at left was barely being used.

Ginnie's mother, a sweet-faced, pudgy little woman, wore a black dress but no veil; she clutched a hanky and the strap of her purse in one hand and with the other held the hand of her son, Roger. Neither Ginnie's mother nor her brother Roger looked anything like her. Mrs. Mullens had a round face, and so did Roger. Same delicate features. Both wore glasses, but Roger's were thick and black-rimmed where his mother's were delicate and wire. Mother and son weighed about the same and were of a similar height and, despite the twenty years between them, could have been older sister and younger brother but for her white hair and his black, sitting there like a plump pair of salt and pepper shakers.

"Mrs. Mullens," I said, standing before her.

She stood and hugged me and looked up at me with a brave smile and red eyes; a whisper of liquor on her breath. "Mal. Oh, Mal, I'm so glad you're here. . . ."

The coffin was nearby; closed. Plenty of flowers, though there had been few visitors. A few relatives—uncles, aunts—were walking around looking at the cards on the flowers, seeing who'd sent what.

"You just missed Jill Forest," she said, sitting down. "She was in you kids' class, wasn't she?"

I nodded, took the chair on the other side of her; Roger looked over at me blankly, like the Pillsbury dough boy.

Roger was two years older than Ginnie, and had always been something of a brain. As smart as Ginnie was, her brother was said to be smarter. Twenty years later, and he hadn't set the world on fire, yet. Last time I talked to him, perhaps ten years ago, he'd been a computer programmer at Maxwell Consultants, an engineering firm.

"Hello, Roger."

"Hello."

"I'm sorry about your loss."

Roger shrugged. "I'm not worried."

"Pardon?"

"I didn't need that job anyway. I was too good for them."

"What are you talking about, Roger?"

Mrs. Mullens, gravely, said, "Maxwell's laid Roger off last month."

Roger said, "What did you think I was talking about?"

I didn't know what to say to that.

Mrs. Mullens smiled like a fairy godmother and patted Roger's arm. "Roger will find something soon, I'm sure."

Something like a smile curled in his pudgy face. "I may go into business for myself. I can write programs with the best of them."

"I'm, uh, sure you can, Roger."

Silence.

Roger stood. "I'm going to catch a smoke, Mom. Be right back."

"That's fine, Roger."

She watched him go, with rheumy eyes. "I wish he wouldn't smoke."

"Is Roger still living at home?"

She smiled just a little, sighed pleasantly. "Yes, and he's a godsend."

"Helps you around the house, you mean."

"Well—he doesn't really have *time* for that. He has to work with his computer. But having his company—just to have him there at mealtime—it means so much. And now with Ginnie gone ... I ... I treasure his company even more." She turned a very serious gaze on me; her eyes were Ginnie's— nothing else about her was Ginnie, just her eyes. "You know, it occurred to me this morning ... thinking about losing Ginnie ... I just take that boy for granted sometimes. I just don't appreciate him like I should."

I tried to think of something polite to say about the fat little bastard and instead said, "I saw Ginnie at the class reunion last month."

"Was that the last time you saw her, Mal?"

"Yes."

No. Last night I'd seen her put into the back of an ambulance. Under a sheet.

"Mal, how were her spirits?"

"Good. I'd say, good. She said she was happy."

"How could she have ..." She let out a confused sigh.

"I don't know. Ginnie didn't seem the sort of person who would take her life."

She looked off somewhere, nowhere, nodding to no one. "Sometimes we don't know people as well as we think we do. As close as Ginnie and I were, I ... I would never have guessed this of her."

I took her hand and squeezed it a little; we

smiled tightly at each other. Blinked our individual tears away.

But Mrs. Mullens was lying. Not to me. Herself.

She and Ginnie had been anything but close. Ginnie had always treated her mom rather callously when we were kids in junior high and high school. Back then I'd found it amusing, being a teenager myself and getting a kick out of seeing anybody get away with talking to a parent like that. Anything to kick authority in the pants.

Now, looking back, I could see Ginnie had treated her mom pretty shabbily.

"We had a special relationship, Ginnie and I," she said. "We didn't see each other often, but when we did it . . . it was *quality* time."

"When did you see her last, Mrs. Mullens?"

She thought about it. "Christmas. No. Not this Christmas, the Christmas before that."

Ginnie lived twenty-some miles from her mother and they hadn't seen each other in over a year.

"She was down for the reunion," I said. "Didn't she stop by. . . ?"

"That was a busy day for her."

I swallowed. "Yeah, that was kind of a frantic weekend."

She dabbed at her eyes with the hanky, glanced toward the coffin, tentatively. "Oh, she and I, we didn't see each other so much, but we talked on the phone, all the time."

"Really."

"Sure. Sometimes she'd call at night and

we'd have mother-and-daughter talks into the wee hours."

I hoped that was true.

What she said next I *knew* was true. She squeezed my hand hard and looked at me harder and said, "A mother and daughter can drift apart, but that doesn't make her any less a daughter ... any less your baby. Does it?"

"No, it doesn't."

And I held her and she cried into my white shirt. I patted her back and said, "There, there." As she drew away I again smelled the alcohol on her breath. An old problem of hers.

I wasn't surprised it was still with her, really; she'd had it ever since I was a kid, her drinking problem. When Ginnie's father was on the road, she would sometimes come over to our house and stay with us, bringing Ginnie along, to try to stay on the wagon with my mother's moral support. But sooner or later, Mrs. Mullens would hit the sauce again, and I knew that was the major reason why Ginnie thought so little of her mom.

Once, in our high school days, I told Ginnie her potsmoking was no different than her mother's drinking and she just laughed and said I was such a square.

"I thought more of her friends would drop by," Mrs. Mullens said, disappointed with the turnout.

"There aren't too many of her old high school classmates still in town. Some of her

Iowa City friends will be at the service tomorrow morning, I'm sure."

"That would be nice. J.T. and Malinda will be here tomorrow. You know J.T., don't you? Ginnie's husband?"

"Yes. And Malinda is Ginnie's daughter."

"That's right. J.T.'s a nice man. He's a poet, you know. I wish things could have worked out for Ginnie and J.T."

"I look forward to meeting Ginnie's daughter."

"Sweet little girl. She's four. Sweet child." She wiped her eyes with the handkerchief again, and clutched her purse and rose, saying, "If you'll excuse me for a moment. I need to take some medicine."

She went off to the restroom. Ninety-proof medicine, no doubt. Whatever got her through this was fine with me.

I went looking for Roger. He was standing out in front, smoking a recently lit cigarette, the pastel floodlights of the funeral home giving him a little color.

"That your second cigarette, Roger?"

"If it is, what concern of yours is it?"

"Your mother could use a little support."

He looked at me with smug distaste. "Who are you to talk? When was the last time you even *saw* my mother? I spend every *day* with her."

"It's cheaper than rent."

"Go to hell."

"You didn't even like your sister much, did you, Roger?"

A convertible rumbled by, a couple of boys in Skol caps, their radio blasting some heavy-metal "song."

"That's my business," Roger said, watching them.

"When did you see her last?"

"Last night," he said, casually.

"Last *night*?"

"That's right."

"How long before she was killed?"

His head swiveled to look at me; eyes like black buttons. "Who says she was killed? The sheriff says it's suicide."

"Nothing's official yet, Roger. When did you see her?"

"Go to hell."

I walked over to him and smiled and put an arm around his shoulder; he looked at me suspiciously.

"Let's be friends, Roger."

"I never liked you and you never liked me, Mallory. Let's leave it that way."

"Fine. But we can at least be polite, can't we?"

"What do you mean by that?"

"I mean, answer my question, or maybe I'll roll you down West Third like a barrel."

He pushed me away. "Leave me alone! I'll—"

"Tell your mother?"

He sucked on the cigarette, nervously. "Why don't you leave? You're not family."

"Tell me about the last time you saw your sister."

"It was after supper. Maybe seven. I was gone by eight. We talked, that's all."

"What about?"

He shrugged. "I told you before I was out of work. I went to Ginnie for some help." Snort. "For all the good it did me."

"What do you mean?"

"I got brains!" he said, poking a thumb at his chest, hard, like that was where he kept them. "She had money. I offered her a business proposition, and she was too stupid to take me up on it."

"What sort of business proposition?"

"Why should I tell you this?"

"Would you rather tell it to Sheriff Brennan?"

His dough boy face went slack with concern. Self-concern. "Do you think she was . . . murdered or something?"

"Or something," I said. "Tell me about the business proposition."

His shoulders sagged. "I've been developing my own computer programs."

"Such as?"

"You wouldn't understand, you dumb ass. Suffice to say I was seeking backing, to package and sell my wares."

"Suffice to say. Why go to Ginnie?"

"She had money! She just sold that shop, didn't she? She had money."

"She turned you down."

That pudgy face turned into a scowl; it was like seeing a Cabbage Patch doll get pissed. "She didn't just turn me down. She laughed at me. Said I was . . . pathetic."

I knew how he felt; she'd called me that once.

"We fought."

"Fought?"

"Don't make anything out of it, Mallory. We had an argument. Words. Like we been having since I was six and she was four, okay? We *never* got along."

"Then why'd you ask her for money?"

He looked shocked. "Hell—family's family, isn't it? Blood's thicker than water."

Ginnie's was; I'd seen some of it at her farmhouse last night.

His cigarette was down to the butt; he tossed it at the street, trailing orange sparks. Another car with boys and heavymetal music rolled by.

"If you were such a great friend of hers," he said, dripping sarcasm, "where were you when our father died?"

That had been last October; I'd been at a convention "I was out of town," I said, feeling a pang of guilt anyway.

"Did you come around and see Mom? Did you go see Ginnie?"

"I sent your mother a card," I said. "And I called Ginnie. If it's any of your business."

"You don't like it so much when somebody asks *you* questions," he said, and waddled inside.

I sat on the steps of the funeral home.

Ginnie's father.

Jack Mullens. What a great, great guy.

Took me fishing once when I was thirteen; let me, a junior-high kid, sit in and play poker with him and his friends, more than once; made me feel like an adult. I could see his blue eyes, under the shock of red hair, in a face full of faded freckles, smiling, the butt of a cigar clenched in his teeth as he studied a hand of poker like it was his private joke on the rest of us. It usually was.

Ginnie and her old man were close, very close; she disdained her mother as an unimaginative housewife, tied to her home and her son and her bottle. A symbol of everything the new liberated female wanted not to be. But Dad, wheeler-dealer Dad, hustler Dad, a born salesman, most of his life spent on the road, he was a guy who knew how to live life to the fullest. He'd died in a head-on collision with a livestock truck; he'd only been going 55, the cops said. That was his age, as well.

I went in and said goodnight to Mrs. Mullens, gave her a kiss on the cheek, smelling "medicine" on her breath, and nodded to her lump of a son. I paused at the casket, the closed casket, but somehow couldn't imagine Ginnie in it.

Then I went home and tried to write, tried to get the new novel going, and couldn't.

I lay in bed thinking about the last time I saw Ginnie, thinking about my class reunion.

9

THE CLASS REUNION HAD BEEN HELD AT THE local Elks Club, a massive two-story brick building facing Mississippi Drive, overlooking Riverview Park, which overlooked a Mississippi River view, as chance would have it. It was a cool June evening, and under a full moon the river looked gray and was stippled with gentle waves; I felt strangely detached. Somewhere between an out-of-body experience, and watching a rerun of a TV show you hadn't much cared for the first time around. I was alone. Most of the people getting out of the cars filling the Elks parking lot were paired off. I wasn't half of a married couple, however; I was a complete single male. Technically complete, anyway.

I felt a little awkward about the whole

thing. I'd purposely missed the ten-year reunion, having just had a rather nasty experience with an old girl friend from my high school days. Actually, she went back to my junior high days, but had haunted me through high school as well. Then, ten years later, she and her larcenous husband reentered my life, and, well—that's another story.

Anyway, on the off chance that Debbie Lee would be at the ten-year reunion, I'd made sure I was out of town that weekend; later I learned that she hadn't attended (probably ducking me just as I was ducking her) but that a number of my old buddies had made a trip back to Port City, some of whom I hadn't seen since graduation. I was sick about missing them, and pledged (to myself, and a few people who checked up on me later to see why I'd stayed away) to attend the fifteenth reunion.

And, so, now I was here. There was to be a dinner, a banquet, so I'd worn a navy sports coat and gray slacks and white shirt, and a skinny red tie I'd had for years, but which was passing these days for "new wave." Even so, I was a little underdressed. It was like a latter-day prom—guys in suits, their "ladies" in gowns, or damn near. There were, of course, a few exceptions; Ginnie, among them, in her layered earth tones and funky jewelry, the late sixties meets Annie Hall in a health food co-op. Her red hair was a mid-sixties shag, and she wore almost no makeup, just freckles and a face that I suddenly realized for the first time in my life was very beautiful. Before this, I'd always looked at it and had just seen Ginnie; now I realized she was a stunning girl. Woman. She hadn't been a girl for a long time, really—not since I was a boy.

"Looks like you're another single-o," she said, finding me in the mob in the wide Elks hallway, slipping her arm in mine. "Let's pair up."

"Why not?" I said, and pecked her on the cheek.

A hundred or so "kids" thirty-three to thirty-five, most of them my former class-mates, were waiting to go into the dining room. The walls herding us in were papered in a garish red with brocade fleur-de-lys; in big fancy gold-filigreed mirrors, we looked back at ourselves and saw how old we were; subdued electric lighting hiding in elaborate glass chandeliers attempted to work a soft-focus magic on us. But it wouldn't take: we just weren't eighteen anymore. We weren't even twenty-five anymore. Nobody thirty-three to thirty-five likes to think it, but we were middle-aged.

"Shit," Ginnie said.

"You're that glad to see me?" I asked.

We were still arm in arm.

She said, "I was just thinking how old we're all looking."

"You look about thirteen."

"It's the freckles. You'd never know I was a thirtyish junkie."

I looked close at her, trying not to seem to be, wondering if she was kidding.

She looked around her, a child taking in her surroundings. "Boy, I haven't been in the Elks Club since the prom. They remodeled since then, didn't they?"

"Appears so. Quite the decorating scheme."

"Early Whorehouse," she smirked, nodding toward the red brocade paper. "I wouldn't be surprised if Dolly Parton came down those stairs with her personality hanging out."

We were in fact at that moment being herded slowly past a wide stairway on which some of our former classmates sat, uncomfortable in their suits and fancy dresses, looking like old kids, but chattering like young ones. The racket in the hallway was less than deafening, but just barely. Faces were overly animated, as current personalities faded and old, younger ones reemerged; the return of youthful personas made the age lines stand out even more.

"Wishing you'd stayed home, Mal?"

I found a smile. "No. I'm getting to see you, aren't I? I don't see Jim Hoffmann or Mike Bloom anywhere, do you?"

"No. I doubt they made it back. Hoff's in Colorado, isn't he? And Bloom's in Council Bluffs or something? A lawyer?"

"Yeah. With a bank, I think. Ron Parker probably won't be here; he's still in the service, running an officer's club in Hawaii. Tough duty, huh? But I wonder if John

Leuck'll make it, and Wheaty, and the rest of the guys."

"They were here at the ten-year," she said. "All except Wheaty—rumor is, he became a circus clown. But that's probably just a story."

Somehow it surprised me she would attend the ten-year reunion—even though here she was at the fifteenth. "So you made the tenth?" I said.

"Sure," she said. "It was a great reunion. Just about everybody was there, except you."

"I wish I'd gone."

"And stayed home tonight."

"Not at all. I'm sure I'll see plenty of the guys."

"Not to mention the gals."

"You forget, Ginnie—I didn't date much in high school."

"Ah, yes—stuck on Debbie Lee. Will she be here tonight?"

I shrugged. "Probably not. She moved to Michigan or Wisconsin or someplace. I get those states mixed up."

"Yeah," Ginnie said, smirking again. "I get states with more than one syllable mixed up all the time, myself."

I grinned at her. "You never change, do you?"

Her smirk turned to a smile; on reflection, I think it may have been a sad one.

"That's not necessarily a compliment, Mal."

"I meant it as such."

"I know. At least you didn't mean it meanly.

But some patterns are tough to break out of, when you've been locked into 'em since you were a kid."

"Such as?"

"Oh, I don't know. How's the writing coming?"

"Changing the subject on me?"

"No—just wondering what a girl has to do to get a book dedicated to her. I was there when it all started, kiddo. I always believed in you, you know."

I sensed she was apologizing again for her long-ago tactless putdown in the cafeteria, but I didn't say as much. Not in so many words, at least.

I just said, "That's nice to know. Thanks, Gin."

"Don't mention it." She stood on her tiptoes; the crowd was slowly moving into the dining room. "Is that Brad Faulkner up ahead?"

I looked, but didn't know why; I hardly knew Faulkner back in school, and wouldn't recognize him today if he came up and introduced himself.

But I said, "I don't know. Maybe."

"I hear he's divorced."

I didn't know he was married.

"No kidding," I said.

She was still on her tiptoes, presumably looking toward Faulkner.

"Tell me something, Ginnie."

"Anything, my sweet. Or anyway, damn near anything."

"How's life treating you these days? ETC.'s must be making you a bundle."

Shrugging, she told me, briefly, about selling out to Caroline Westin.

"I thought you'd hang onto that place forever," I said.

"Nothing lasts forever," she said. She assumed a toughguy, side-of-the-mouth expression. " 'Live fast, die young, and have a good-looking corpse.' "

"Willard Motley, 1947," I said.

"Right! *Knock On Any Door*! Great book! You remembered that?"

"Ginnie, I gave you that book."

Her smile melted. "That's right," she said, strangely sad. "How could I forget?"

"Ginnie, it's no big deal. We both turned each other onto a lot of books."

"He was black, did you know that?"

"Who?"

"Motley. Willard Motley."

"Yeah, actually, I did know that. He usually wrote about white people, though."

"It was the times," she said. "He was better off passing for white, in his way. He could get his book read more widely, I guess. It's better now, don't you think?"

"How do you mean?"

"The world's improved. Things have changed for the better, a little."

"Maybe, a little."

"It wasn't all just talk."

The crowd was moving faster now, toward our meal, and though I was following along like a good sheep, I wasn't able to follow Ginnie's line of thought.

"What are you getting at, Gin?"

"Just thinking about the sixties, those days. The things we marched for, and protested about; things really did change, we really did stop a war."

"I suppose."

We were jostled close together; her eyes looked wide and blue and empty and yet fathomless. Freckles or not, she looked suddenly old. I didn't know she was the oldest person in the room, that she had a month to live, when she said, "I'm dreamin', aren't I? It really isn't much better. We didn't really accomplish much, did we?"

"We're just another generation, Ginnie. Like most generations, we thought we were special."

"And weren't?"

"Maybe we were. Maybe we weren't. But I know one thing we most certainly were."

"Yeah? What?"

"Kids."

They alternated serving plates of rare roast beef with well-done, giving you the opportunity to barter with your neighbor; we sat in the huge dining room, passing plates around, children in coats and ties and fancy dresses, exchanging food as if in the high school cafeteria. ("Trade you my dessert for your roll.") Like all children, we weren't content with what we were given; we had to change things to our liking.

"You know, we did change things," I said to Ginnie, who was sitting beside me, with whom I'd swapped my well-done beef for her rare (she wasn't eating the beef anyway, as she was strictly veggie).

"What?" she said, through a mouthful of lettuce. I'd given her my salad for her cherry cobbler. She was busy eating and had already forgotten our "heavy" conversation out in the herd.

"We changed the world," I said, "but not to make things better for the common man. Just for ourselves."

That got her going.

"What about Vietnam?" she said. "It wasn't rich kids dying over there, you know."

"No, it was some middle-class kids and lots of poor kids. White and black alike. *Most* males of the 'love' generation were at least *threatened* by that war, Ginnie. Guys my age were against the war because they were afraid of getting drafted. So they protested. A purely selfish move."

Smiling with cute smugness, Ginnie pointed a lettuce-tipped fork at me, thinking she had me. "You protested *after* you went to Vietnam. After you got back. Was *that* a purely selfish move?"

"A partly selfish ove. We were after better benefits from the V.A., as well as wanting to end the war. And, besides, I wasn't a kid anymore."

"So automatically you were unselfish, being an adult."

"That's a position I'd rather not try to defend," I said, working on the lumpy mashed potatoes; the dark gravy was also lumpy. More cafeteria nostalgia.

She sighed. "You're right. Why argue about it? We were as self-centered a generation as this self-centered country has ever known."

"You obviously haven't heard of MTV."

With a gentle, short-lived laugh, she said, "This generation isn't as smug as we were. They don't think they know it all, like we did."

"Unfortunately, they don't seem to *want* to know it all, either. They don't seem to want to know anything, much."

"You're sounding like an old man, Mal."

"There's a reason for that. Ginnie, tell me. Are you happy?"

She was working on her mashed potatoes now. She shrugged, forced a little smile. "I'm happy. Business is good—though I haven't made my million yet."

"What the hell," I said.

"Goals were made to be ignored," she said, shrugging yet again. You shrug a lot at class reunions; people ask you that sort of question.

"Or," she said, "anyway, adjusted."

"Is money still your *main* goal?"

Shrug.

"What about your personal life, Gin? How goes it?"

She told me she was married, but not living with her husband; she gave me no details, other than she had a little girl four, named Malinda—Mal for short. And so on.

Upstairs, after the banquet, in the ballroom there was a dance. Crusin', a popular local oldies band, began cranking 'em out: "Wooly Bully," "Time Won't Let Me," "Don't Let Me Be Misunderstood." They had a good, big, authentic sound, but they were loud, and another sign of how old we were getting was that some of us complained. Not me. I just sat out in the bar and drank too many Pabsts and talked to everybody I hadn't known very well in high school but who suddenly were back-slapping old pals. My whole crowd had stayed home—in their new homes; out-of-state success stories, they left me here alone to swap memories with a guy from study hall named Joey Something, who if I remember right said nary a word for two semesters, and now was the successful—and vocal—owner of three gas stations; half a dozen heavyset women who turned out to be "whatever happened to" half a dozen svelte attractive girls, former cheerleaders, prom queens and the like; half a dozen svelte attractive women who had once been wallflowers and, having bloomed late, were tasting the revenge of living well, and thinly; a great big fat guy who used to be a little bitty skinny guy, and grew after graduation, in various directions; several people who told me who they were, and summoned a mental picture of who they'd been, but I'll be damned if I could spot who they used to be in the

faces they wore now; a good number of
people who hadn't changed much, really,
though potbellies were the plague of the
males, all in all the women holding up
better. It was an evening of cruel thoughts
("Thank God I didn't end up with *her*—to
think she turned me down for the prom!"),
bittersweet regrets ("Why didn't I date *her*—
she liked me, and I shunned her, and now
she's *beautiful*!"), petty jealousy ("How could
a jerk like him end up with a dish like
her?"), pure jealousy ("He must be worth half
a million by now—and I gave the son of a
bitch his *history* answers!"), and genuine
sorrow ("I wish John were alive and here . . .").

Ginnie had split off from me as soon as we
got upstairs, wanting to go in and dance; the
blare of the music had sent me to this small
table in the bar area, where friends came
and went, and most of the evening I spent
with Michael Lange, a guy I'd been in chorus
with. He used to wear a suit to school and
carry a briefcase; he'd left the briefcase
home tonight, and brought a mustache, but
otherwise looked the same—of course, he'd
looked thirty-five in high school, so maybe
we just caught up with him. He was into
computers, but I liked him anyway, though I
understood little of what he said; as the
evening wore on, and Michael drank a few
too many Dos Equis, he began understanding
little of what he was saying himself. No
matter. I wasn't listening.

I was watching as Ginnie, over by the

ladies restroom, was having a rather heated argument with an attractive woman whom I hadn't placed. Ginnie was pointing a finger at the woman, and the woman was pointing a finger back; they weren't shouting, but it was intense.

Their arguing had caught my attention, but it was the woman who maintained that attention. She was about five-six, had black punky hair and cute features and a sweet little shape; she was not wearing a prom gown, but a wide-shouldered designer number, Zebra stripes above, black skirt below, really striking. She had red lipstick so dark it was damn near black, and green glittery eyeshadow.

"Who *is* that?" I asked Michael.

In a tone that sought to be pompous, but had dos Dos Equis ago turned just plain silly, Michael said, "How should I know? Am I her keeper?"

"Could that be Jill Forest?"

"I'm afraid I can't see Jill Forest for the trees."

"Right, Michael. Have another beer."

It *was* Jill Forest, but she was gone now, and so was Ginnie, back in the ballroom.

I'd dated Jill a few times in high school day, but she'd been a quiet girl, and her parents had been strict, and, for reasons that now escaped me, we'd never clicked. She'd been too cute to be mousy, but, even so, this was a shock: Jill Forest a trendy stand-out in a crowd where it wasn't unusual to see a woman wearing the same hairstyle she'd worn to the senior prom. On the other hand, I was wearing the same tie I'd worn to the prom, so who was I to condescend? I was just a cheap bastard, trying to pass for trendy.

I spent the rest of the evening looking for Jill out of the corner of either eye, and not seeing her.

I did see Ginnie, though we didn't speak again that evening. She was spending a lot of time at a table for two in the ballroom, huddling with a dark, not particularly handsome man who I took to be Brad Faulkner. A little drunk, she seemed to be flirting outrageously—and he seemed to be liking it, giving her a shy smile while she did almost all the talking. They were dancing slow, to "Easy to Be Hard," a song from *Hair*, when I left around midnight. Walking home, leaving my car in the Elks parking lot. I was damn near sober by he time I got home, and lay awake till two wondering why Ginnie had spent so much time with Faulkner, a guy I didn't remember being anybody she had dated or run around with or anything way back when. It seemed strange.

A month later, with Ginnie dead, I was again awake at two in the morning, and it seemed even stranger.

10

PORT CITY CABLEVISION LURKED BEHIND THE massive modern Community College library, across an access road; behind Cablevision was sprawling Weed Park (named after a guy named "Weed," so help me), making quite the impressive back yard for so undistinguished a structure, a one-story white frame building with satellite dishes growing around it, like strange mushrooms.

I was not here to complain about the service, even though ever since they added the Disney Channel and scrambled it, the channels on either side were constantly visited by a rolling tweed pattern. One of those disrupted channels was the all-Spanish network, and the other was twenty-four-hour stock quotations; since I was not a wealthy Mexican investor, I could live without either.

I was here to see Jill Forest. This morning, at the inappropriately sunny graveside services at Greenwood Cemetery, she had been there, wearing a black suit and dark glasses, the only other person there besides me remotely Ginnie's age; none of the Iowa City friends had made it, Flater and Sturms included. Oddly absent too were John "J.T." O'Hara, the hippie poet Ginnie married, and their daughter Malinda; Mrs. Mullens had told me at the funeral home she expected them, but I didn't see them. Sheriff Brennan was on hand, though, and I asked him if he knew Jill, saying, "I used to go to school with her, but had no idea she was still in town."

"She isn't still in town," he said. "She's *back* in town."

Turned out Jill had been in the cable TV business for five or six years, going into communities like ours and putting things in motion for a year or so, then moving on. Perhaps it was a coincidence that one of her myriad jobs had been Port City, her old home town. Or maybe not. That was one of the things I planned to ask her.

So far all I'd asked her, on the phone, was if she remembered me, and if she might entertain an invitation for lunch. In a pleasant but businesslike manner, she'd said yes to both.

Now here I was at Cablevision, going in

the side studio entrance as she'd instructed
me, wondering what to say to the shy girl in
Junior Miss dresses I'd dated in high school
who had become a lady executive in outfits
by Kamali. I, by the way, was not going the
Bilko and camouflage route today—as at the
funeral, I wore a black polo shirt and gray
slacks, the same slacks I'd worn to the
reunion. The day was warm, and I'd rather
worn shorts, but I needed to make a better
impression than that on Jill, or anyway I
wanted to.

The air conditioning inside Cablevision was
welcome. A modest studio with a modest
glassed-in booth was at my right as I walked
down a narrow hall to a door with JILL
FOREST, STATION MANAGER on it; that
her job was temporary was indicated by her
name and rank being on a sliding piece of
plastic that fit in steel grooves on the door.

I knocked.

"Yes," her voice said, noncommittally.

I spoke to the door. "It's Mal."

"Come in," her voice said, just as noncommittally.

Not that it was an unpleasant voice; it was
a warm mid-range voice that had to work at
sounding all business. But she managed it.

Feeling a little intimidated and not really
knowing why, I went in.

It wasn't a big office; thinking of her as an
executive was an exaggeration. And she wasn't
wearing Kamali or any other designer clothes.
Just a simple white blouse with a black dress

(she stood as I came in) with a geometric copper necklace the only new-wave fashion touch of the day. Her short black hair still had a vaguely punk look to it, and her lipstick was redder than Dracula's wildest dreams. Her eye makeup was subdued compared to at the reunion, though; with those cornflower blue eyes, who needed it?

And she had a great tan.

"You have a great tan," I said.

I couldn't help myself.

She sat back down. "Is that what you wanted to talk about, Mal, after all this time? My tan?" Her tone wasn't exactly unfriendly. It wasn't exactly friendly, either.

"That was dumb," I said, sitting down myself. "I don't know why I said it."

She shrugged, her expression revealing nothing. "I don't have that much of a tan. I've always been on the dark side. Don't you remember?"

That was the problem: I didn't remember. I'd gone out with her back in school, yes; more than once—and then called it off. I didn't remember her looking even remotely this good. I was thirty-four and unmarried and here was one of the first of many prize catches I'd foolishly let get away over the years. Feel free to kick me.

"Sure I remember," I said.

Now she smiled, just a little. "You don't, do you? I didn't make much of an impression on you when we were kids."

"That's not true! We used to go out, and have a lot of fun."

"We went out two times, and probably said ten words to each other, total. We did not have a lot of fun. We didn't even have a little fun."

I sighed. "We didn't, did we?"

She shrugged again, looking at a desk piled with neatly stacked work. "I was quiet, then. Like they say in the old movies: too quiet."

"Your parents kept you on a pretty short leash."

Something flickered in her eyes, but she kept her face impassive. "Maybe that's because I was a 'dog,' hmm?"

"I didn't mean it like that. You were a cute kid; I never thought of you like that, ever. But your parents were the have-her-home-by-ten-on-weekend-nights types. Uh, how are your folks, by the way?"

"Dead."

She meant that to shock me. I didn't say anything.

She said, "How are yours?"

"My what?"

"Parents."

"Oh. Dead."

I meant that to shock her. She didn't say anything.

Then she smiled a genuine smile. The white teeth in her dark face, like the light blue eyes, made quite a contrast; this was one striking-looking woman.

"Why am I giving you a hard time?" she said. "You were always nice to me, Mal. It's just that I wanted more than nice."

"What do you mean?"

"I had a monster crush on you, all through high school. When you finally asked me out, I almost died with joy. Then when the time came, I got nervous, and clammed up, and blew my chance."

"We went out more than once, remember."

"I blew it both times."

"If you'd blown it both times," I said, with just a hint of Groucho, "I'd have kept going out with you."

"Mal!" she said, with a shocked smile, a teenager pretending to be more embarrassed than she was. "How can you say such a thing?"

"I'm just one crazy kid, I guess. Are you married, Jill?"

"No."

"Would you like to he?"

Now she really smiled. "Part of me wishes you weren't kidding."

"Part of me isn't kidding," I said. "Where do you want to have lunch?"

She felt like walking, so we strolled outside and wandered out into the sunny day and down the hill into Weed Park. The lagoon was at the bottom, and a mother and her two kids, a boy and a girl both under ten, were feeding bread crumbs to the ducks. We went up another hill, past some tennis courts, toward the swimming pool, where kids were splashing and hollering, making a pleasant racket. There was a hot dog stand across from the pool.

We ate our hot dogs with plenty of mustard and not much conversation, at a picnic table in a little area by a cannon on a bluff overlooking the river. We had the table to ourselves, though the sound of a baseball game—kids again—intruded, in a good-natured way. Yes, it was warm, but there was a breeze. A warm breeze, but a breeze. It was nice to be alive.

We were not ignoring each other by not speaking; we were just paying attention to our hot dogs. Priorities. I was carefully trying not to get any mustard on my black shirt, not wanting to look like a jerk in front of her; she was waging a similar battle where her white blouse was concerned. Success met us both, and we began talking, nibbling at potato chips and sipping cups of pop.

"I noticed you at Ginnie's services this morning," she said. "Otherwise I don't know if I'd have agreed to see you."

"Oh? Am I that bad a memory?"

Small laugh. "No, you're just one of those frustrating high school memories that haunts a person till his or her dying day. Truth is, I'd have accepted your invitation, under about any conditions. I've been waiting for this for longer than I can remember."

That puzzled me. "Waiting for what?"

Her chin crinkled as she smiled with some embarrassment. "I always wanted to show you what I'd become."

"You mean beautiful? Or a very together, intelligent businesswoman?"

She smiled tightly and viewed me through slitted eyes. "All of that," she said. "And more."

"I'd welcome more."

"You're flirting with me, aren't you, Mal?"

"Yeah, I seem to be. So?"

"So," she said. "I seem to like it."

We finished our pop and walked over by the cannon, which was pointed out toward the Mississippi, which looked blue but choppy today.

And I'll be damned if she wasn't holding my hand.

I peered into those cornflower eyes, an incongruous blue in so dark a face and wondered if in her expression I could read permission to kiss her. Her chin tilted up a little, and I took that to mean yes.

It was a short, sweet, moist little kiss that tasted slightly of mustard. It was also in the Top Ten Kisses of this or any generation.

"See what you missed?" she said, and turned and walked away.

I followed like a puppy. "How was I to know you were going to turn into Pat Benatar's older, better-looking sister?"

"What you mean *older*, paleface?"

I caught up with her. "You're my age, aren't you? Thirtyfour?"

"Thirty-three," she said, "and holding."

"Slow down."

"Mal," she said, not slowing down, "this has been pleasant, but I really have to get back. I only take a half-hour lunch."

"Whoa. I didn't call you just so you could have your revenge on me."

She stopped, poked a tongue in her cheek. "My revenge?"

"Sure. You turned beautiful purely to spite me, right? Just to rub my face in it."

"You wish," she said, moving quickly on again, but smiling.

I reached for her arm. "Hold it, hold it, hold *on!*"

She held on; stood with hands on hips, with mock impatience. From the evil little smile she wasn't quite suppressing, I knew she was getting a real kick out of making me jump through hoops. The hell of it was, I was getting a real kick out of jumping through.

Nonetheless, I said, "I love fencing with you, Jill, and I would be glad to spend a lot of time over the next hundred years or so doing just that. But I did call you for a serious reason. Not just old times."

Her smile disappeared. "What, then?"

"Ginnie," I said. "I'm trying to find out what happened to Ginnie."

Her brow knit in lack of understanding. "She . . . killed herself, didn't she?"

"Maybe."

"Maybe?"

"Please. Sit down." We were near yet another picnic table. We sat. She was next to me, this time, not across from me. I held her hand, platonically, as I explained that Sheriff Brennan had asked me to ask around a little, due to Ginnie's "suicide" having some suspicious over- and undertones. Though I'd spent all day yesterday talking to people about Ginnie, I had confided this to none of them. Just Jill. Don't ask me why.

"I don't know how I can help you," she said. "I hadn't seen Ginnie since the reunion. In fact, we had a little falling out there. An argument."

"I see." I didn't mention to Jill that I knew about the argument already; I didn't want to make her feel like a suspect. Not so much because I wanted to shrewdly manipulate her into telling me things that she might otherwise withhold; but because I didn't want to get on her bad side. I wanted her to like me. Sue me.

Jill's brow furrowed deeper as she dug into her memories, some of them painful, apparently. "I moved back to Port City six months ago, and when I heard Ginnie was still in the area, I looked her up. We were good friends in high school . . . you didn't know that, did you, Mal? You two weren't as close in high school as you were when you were younger— sharing books, talking out under the stars . . . does it surprise you I know about that? You forget—I had that monster crush on you and I always was one to do my homework; I found out everything I could about you, and Ginnie was a good source. She used to say you were like brother and sister. She really loved you. I think it hurt her after you stopped talking to her that time she insulted you."

"You know about that, too?"

"I don't know what it was she said to you, but it must've been bad. She had a childish streak, always did. She would say or try anything, just for the hell of it, to see how it played. And sometimes she lost. You were a major loss for her, Mal."

"So you got back in touch with her when you came back to town."

"Yes. Yes. We were seeing each other every now and then over these last six months— usually we'd share lunch in Iowa City and gab about old times. And she'd kid me—she couldn't *believe* I missed the 'revolution.'"

"What do you mean?"

She half smiled. "I was never a hippie. I went to the University of Iowa, majored in business. I studied hard—I wanted to get out of this state."

"Iowa, you mean?"

"Iowa, and the *general* state I was in. A nobody, a nothing, a female nerd. So I dug in and studied, to make something out of nothing. I was in the library for such lengths of time that I didn't hear about Kent State till they shut the school down and pulled me out of the stacks and sent me packing."

"You said you were in the school of business—did you know Caroline Westin?"

"Not well. She was Ginnie's partner in ETC.'s, right?"

"Right. And squeezed Ginnie out apparently, just recently."

Jill considered that. "I don't know. I think Ginnie was ready to get out from under all that anyway. She told me she was sick and tired of business. She seemed frustrated, worn down by it."

"Maybe that was Caroline Westin putting the squeeze on."

"Maybe. But I don't think so."

"What was your argument about?"

"At the reunion? Oh, she'd been talking, the last few times I saw her, about going to Las Vegas again. She had something of a thing for gambling ... I don't know if you knew that, but she did. I'd almost call it an addiction."

"You would."

"Yes—the only things she wanted to talk about when we'd get together were A, gambling; B, her daughter; and C, old times. Those were her concerns in her last days."

Her last days. That had a chilling ring to it.

"So," I said, "you argued about her gambling?"

"Specially this 'one last Vegas score' she'd been talking about. She was going to take everything she had and let it ride."

"Go for broke."

"Go for broke, indeed."

That sounded like Ginnie, all right.

I said, "Did you and Ginnie ever talk about drugs?"

"No. She knew better than that."

"How so?"

"I never was into dope when I was a kid. I did some coke when I was in my New York period, going trendy in SoHo, around six years ago, but I got turned off to that scene quick. Saw some friends ruin themselves and their lives by letting their coke spoons lead 'em around by the nose. The first lunch Ginnie and I had together after I came back, this all came up in conversation, so she never showed that side of herself to me."

"Well, that side of her was there."

"I'm sure it was. But I doubt she was using anything much."

"Yeah. Me, too. Her addiction lay elsewhere."

"Right," she said, nodding, "and that's why we fought at the reunion. I was trying to talk her out of her 'last' big Vegas fling, and she was telling me it was none of my business. None of my 'fucking business,' to be exact."

"Tact was never Ginnie's long suit."

Jill looked sad. "Oh, I don't know. It could be, if she was in the right frame of mind. She could be a sweet, thoughtful kid, when she put her mind to it."

"Jill, at the reunion Ginnie was dancing with this guy Brad Faulkner, remember him?"

She nodded.

"She was hanging all over him," I said. "Why? It's not like she was thick with him back in high school or anything. . . ."

She smiled privately. "A lot you know."

"What do you mean?"

"She went out with him her junior and senior year. They sort of went steady."

"I never knew about it."

"Few people did. They ran with different crowds, and there was a religious problem—his parents were Mormon or something, and, anyway, they used to sneak around. Go to the drive-in on weekends and stuff."

Funny. Now Jill was talking like a kid—"went steady," "weekends and stuff"; smooth professional woman of the world Jill. Funny how who you were in high school stays inside you, and can jump out over the years and take control any old time.

"I think Brad was really thrown by Ginnie coming onto him," she said. "He's still very straight, I hear, though he did get divorced last year. He lost a child in some sort of accident, and it broke up the marriage, or so I was told."

"*Who* told you?"

"Ginnie, actually. She'd been checking up on him."

"Why?"

"I don't know. She was kind of obsessed with her past; otherwise, why would she have lunch with me every week or so, and just hash over old memories? I didn't mind—I liked Ginnie's company. She was bright, and funny, and an old, good friend, always lots of fun. But on the other hand, always a little sad, too, don't you think?"

"I don't know," I admitted. "I didn't see much of her in recent years."

"Oh," she said, getting it suddenly. "This is guilt you're working through, here. You feel guilty about not seeing more of her, living so close up in Iowa City and all."

I didn't deny it.

"Whatever is motivating you," she said, "I'm glad you're looking into this. Ginnie may have been melancholy, but I don't see her for a suicide. She had suicidal tendencies, like her gambling—but I just can't see her putting a gun to her head. It just wasn't in her. If you ask me, you should talk to this Brad Faulkner."

"Oh really?"

"Really. I stopped at the Sports Page after the reunion, and Brad and Ginnie were there together."

The Sports Page was an all-night restaurant out by the Shopping mall.

"So what?" I said.

"So they had a rip-roarin' fight. If you think Ginnie and *I* were arguing—and that's why you wanted to talk to me today, right, I'm a suspect, correct?—Well, you should've seen her and Brad shouting at each other; and then he stormed out of there. Funny thing, though."

"What?"

"He was crying."

11

TRU-TEST HARDWARE WAS A BIG ONE-STORY brown brick building on the slope of First Street, where East Hill falls toward the business district, almost directly opposite the toll bridge across the Mississippi. The place was only a few blocks from where I lived, and I'd stopped in from time to time for some screws (no jokes, please) or fuses or light bulbs; but I wasn't what you'd call a regular customer. I wasn't a regular customer at any hardware store, actually, being to Do-It-Yourselfing what Liberace is to pro football.

Still, I'd been in the store often enough for it to come as something of a sunprise to me to learn that Brad Faulkner, former classmate of mine, was the manager of Tru-Test, a piece of information Jill Forest had passed along. It was now mid-afternoon, and I hoped to find Faulkner among the hammers and nails, in what proved to be a busy store.

I did.

The tall, dark, lumpy-faced Faulkner stood in white smock with Tru-Test circular red logo on the front, as well as green badge with his name and the word "Manager" underneath; his slacks were shiny black and so was his hair. He was standing by a display of popcorn poppers, a clipboard in his hands, checking his stock.

I approached and he sensed me there, spoke without looking at me, smiled the same way.

"Can I help you?" His smile was automatic and meant nothing more than customer service.

"Brad, my name's Mallory—went to school together. Remember?"

Now he looked at me, face tensing. I had put my hand out for him to shake; he took it without enthusiasm.

"I remember you," he said. "But we weren't exactly friends, were we?"

I shrugged; smiled. "We weren't exactly enemies either."

He and his clipboard turned back to the popcorn poppers. In a voice that was almost a whisper, he said, "We weren't exactly anything."

"Faulkner, I . . ."

He glanced back at me, his lip gently sneering. "What happened to 'Brad'?"

"Look, I feel awkward about this, too—I know we weren't good friends or anything. I don't know *what* to call you, exactly—I usually don't call people my own age I went to high school with 'mister,' do you?"

"No," he said, looking at the poppers, jotting notes on a page on the clipboard, "but I don't feel awkward about finding something to call you. You're a busybody."

I resisted the urge to hook my thumbs in my belt and say, *Them's fightin' words, podner.*

Instead I just said, "I've had harsher reprimands in my time. But why do you consider me a 'busybody'?"

He turned and looked at me; he had a couple inches on me, and was fairly sturdy —no middle-age spread at all. "You're asking around about Ginnie Mullens, aren't you?"

"Who told you that?"

"I don't have to tell you anything. I don't have to talk to you at all." He poked me in the chest with a thick forefinger; he was trembling just a little, but with anger, not fear. His voice was soft, however, when he added: "If you aren't a customer, I'd prefer you leave."

"You've probably got a dozen customers in the store right now, Brad, old classmate o' mine. Perhaps a few more. How would it look if this turned into a scene?"

"It's not going to turn into a scene."

"That's fine with me. All I want is to ask you a few questions."

His jaw muscles tensed. "About Ginnie Mullens."

"About Ginnie Mullens."

"Let's step outside."

"Hey, Brad—there's no need for that—"

"To talk. Let's step outside to talk."

He wasn't getting tough, after all; he just wanted to be out of earshot of his customers and employees. Fair enough. We sat in the front seat of my Firebird for further privacy; I even rolled up the windows and started the car to get the air conditioner going. I'm nothing if not a gracious host.

"I'm sorry Ginnie Mullens is dead," he said, gazing forward, the impassive reflection of his impassive face staring back at him in the windshield. "But she really didn't have much to do with my life."

"Your *recent* life."

He nodded; there was something quietly dignified in that lumpy face—that sort of David Hartman ugliness that some women find appealing. Another of the many mysteries of Woman I'll never solve.

Going on the record, he said, "Ginnie Mullens and I went together in high school."

"Secretly."

With a barely perceptible shrug, he said, "Some people knew. Close friends knew." He turned and with deadpan irony added, "I'm surprised you didn't know, being so close to Ginnie Mullens and all."

"Why do you always use both her names? Ginnie Mullens this, Ginnie Mullens that. Why the formality?"

"No reason."

"You're trying to maintain distance between you and her, somehow, for some reason, aren't you? Why?"

Instead of answering, he looked at me like I was one of the popcorn poppers he was inventorying and said, "You write books, don't you?"

"That's right."

He laughed with faint contempt, looked forward again.

I tried to dish some back at him. "What's wrong, Brad? Don't you read books?"

"Not that mystery junk. I read nonfiction."

"Here I figured you more the Bible type."

He turned to me, smiled faintly. "That's what I said: nonfiction."

Like my parked car, my engine was on, but I wasn't getting anywhere.

"Look," I said. "I don't mean to pry into your personal life. But somebody we both cared about, once, has recently died. I'm examining the circumstances of her death, for personal reasons. Trying to understand what brought her ... her promising young life to an early end. So I'm talking to some of her friends, hoping to find ... well, some insights."

"Why talk to me? Ginnie Mullens and I are ancient history."

"Ginnie Mullens is history, all right. And you're part of it."

"Ancient history, I said."

"Not so ancient. Our fifteenth reunion last month?"

This time his shrug was easily perceptible. "What of it?"

"You saw her there."

"I saw a lot of people there. You included, I believe."

"You didn't dance with *me*, Brad."

He looked at me with undisguised disgust, but his voice remained controlled. "She was an old girl friend. We danced. We talked about old times." He began to open the car door. "Now, if you don't mind, I'd like to get back inside . . ."

"Please, Faulkner. Brad. Humor me for a couple more minutes."

He sighed heavily, shut the door. Turned his stare forward again.

"At the reunion, you and Ginnie talked all evening. Without meaning to pry, I'd like to ask if anything the two of you spoke about might have been upsetting to her."

"Without meaning to pry," he said with dry sarcasm.

"They say she committed suicide, you know."

His dark face whitened.

"Did I strike a nerve, Brad?"

"Don't be foolish."

"Are you afraid what you argued about may have upset her so badly she took her life?"

He moved around in the seat. "Who says we argued? And the reunion was a month before; why would anything we talked about then cause her to ... take her life, a month later? Don't be foolish."

Plenty of people saw you arguing at that restaurant, the Sports Page, Brad. And if Ginnie's life was in general disaray your confrontation with her could have been one of several straws that broke the camel's back."

He rubbed his forehead with one hand, as if he were trying to wipe off a deep stain. "I wouldn't like to think that. Despite ..."

"You wouldn't like to think you were part of what might have caused her to kill herself, you mean?"

"N-no."

"*Despite* something, you said. Despite, what?"

He looked out his side window, the back of his head to me as he spoke. "Old business."

"Old business?"

Now he looked toward me, but seemed to look past me, rather than at me. "My little boy was drowned last year, did you know that?"

It was like taking a blow, hearing him say that. His eyes were pools of pain; I hadn't noticed it before, but they were.

I said, "I ... I'd heard something to that effect, but ... look, I'm very, very sorry."

"He was eight. A quiet little boy. Not very athletic. An average student. He collected stamps. Nothing remarkable about him. Except that he was my son and he meant more to me than . . ." Something caught in his voice.

I didn't know why my questioning him about Ginnie had dredged this up, but nonetheless I found myself apologizing. "Brad, I'm sorry . . . I didn't mean to . . ."

He looked toward me; beyond me. "He was our only one, Seth was. We wanted more, but none came. She blamed me."

I didn't say anything, just sat there feeling embarrassed, letting this run its course.

"He couldn't swim," he said, with an odd, mirthless Smile. "Alice was against it. She didn't even like me having a boat."

He wasn't looking at me; he was looking toward the bridge. Toward the Mississippi. The river.

"And he drowned one day. We were out . . ."

I touched his arm. "Don't."

He looked at me; the pools of pain had overflowed, though his face remained impassive, making wet trails across the lumpy, dark, dignified face.

"Ginnie Mullens was a long time ago," he said. "And I really don't want to talk about it." But he didn't reach for the door.

The "she" in his story, Alice, was his divorced wife, of course. And some other things were falling into place in my mind, as well. . . .

I said, "You're a religious man, aren't you, Brad?"

He nodded.

"You had a strict upbringing. Your parents were very devout in their faith, raised you the same. And that caused problems for you when you and Ginnie were going together. Didn't it?"

He nodded again.

"She was a wild girl," I said, "Ginnie Mullens. And you were a teenage boy with the normal teenage urges."

He put his hand over his face, elbow leaned against the dash.

"She was, even then, a hippie. Sex and drugs and rock 'n' roll. I bet that drove your parents crazy."

"It drove me crazy," he said. "God forgive us both."

"I was a close friend of Ginnie's," I said. "I didn't know about her and you, but I knew about many, many private things in Ginnie's life."

He looked at me sharply; his hand had smeared the tears, so that his whole face seemed damp now, like somebody who'd been caught in the rain.

Remembering those nights out under the stars, when Ginnie and I shared secrets, I said, "I know about the abortion she had her junior year."

He swallowed.

"You were the father," I said, "weren't you?"

Another tear trailed down the mask.

I went on. "Ginnie, in that patented, tactless, sometimes cruel manner of hers, brought it up, that long-ago abortion, and rubbed it in your face at the reunion. That's why you fought. That's why you . . ." I didn't finish it: *cried when you stormed out of the Sports Page.*

He stared ahead.

"With the recent loss of your son," I said, carefully, trying to avoid speaking in a tactless, cruel manner myself, "what she said hurt you. Hurt you deep."

He said nothing.

"My question is *how* deep? She may have been murdered, Brad. I believe Ginnie *was* murdered."

That stunned him; he looked at me with wide, red eyes, and a mouth hanging open to where I could count the silver fillings. Seven.

He said, "Murdered?"

"I'm almost sure of it. Where were you the night she died?"

"Alone," he said.

Some alibi.

"But I would never take a life." He winced, possibly thinking of his son. "Knowingly," he amended.

"Did you hate Ginnie Mullens?"

He didn't answer.

I tried again: "Did you hate her?"

He whipped around and grabbed me by the shirt. "Yes!" His eyes were red and fierce and his teeth were clenched and his breath smelled of Listerine; the pores in his nose were large.

"Jesus Christ," I said, scared shitless.

It must've been the right thing to say, because then he let go of me.

"Hated her, yes ..." Leaning against the side door, getting as far away from me as he could without getting out of the car, he said, "But not enough to ... kill her."

"Somebody hated her that much."

"Not me. Only ... only that night ... when she told me."

"Told you what?"

He looked at me with eyes so haunted I saw them in my sleep for months after.

He said, "That she had aborted our child. Sixteen years ago. That I'd had *another* child, sixteen years ago ... and lost him, too."

"She ... she never told you?"

Fists in his lap, shaking. "Not in high school, she didn't. Not until the reunion, last month. In that restaurant."

"My God."

"God. She's in His hands now. Most likely she knows eternal damnation, for what she did. But I don't wish it on her."

"Eternal damnation, you mean."

"Right," he said. And without a trace of sarcasm he said, "Believe me, hell on earth is bad enough."

And he got out of my car and, a figure in a ghost white smock, disappeared into the hardware store.

12

I WAS IN BED WITH JILL FOREST.

I hadn't planned it that way, I swear to you. Not that I'm apologizing, and I'm certainly not complaining. But just because I'd asked her to come to my place for supper—rather than take her out to a restaurant—didn't mean I had any underlying intentions. Or is that underlaying?

Well, here we were, both embarrassed about it; sitting up in my bed, a pale blond art deco piece circa 1933 that I bought at a yard sale, both not knowing quite what to say to each other. We didn't know each other well enough for this to have happened. We'd dated those two times in high school, so you could say we'd known each other for twenty years, but there was the little matter of fifteen years since we'd last seen one another.

She was smoking, which at least gave her something to do with her hands. I just sat with a pillow propped behind me, sneaking looks at her, a beautiful dark-skinned woman with short punky black hair and cornflower blue eyes given a dreamy unreality by the half-light of the scented candle glowing atop the pale blond matching chest of drawers at my left. She was on my right. Smoking. Or did I say that?

"I'm very embarrassed," I said. Admitting it.

She smiled a little. "Me, too."

"I didn't mean for this to happen."

She cocked her head, curiously, the smile fading just a bit.

"Are you sorry?"

"No! No. It was terrific."

And it had been terrific. She'd dropped by for a late supper around nine, after a city council meeting at which she'd announced a projected rate hike for the cable system, looking a little weary from the battle that followed, but sultry, alluring, in a clingy blue dress the color of her eyes and a lot of makeup and no hose. I'd cooked pasta for her, dazzled her with my homemade sauce, wooed her with red wine, garlic bread (not much garlic, though, mostly bread) and spumoni ice cream. (This is one of three dinners I taught myself to prepare for company, preferably female; otherwise, as a chef, I know everything there is to know about frozen food and a microwave.)

I'd shown her around my little house. She'd been amused by my eccentricities—the Seeburg 200 jukebox stocked mostly with Bobby Darin records, the Bally pinball machine with its garish lit-up illustrations of Chicago gangsters and their bosomy molls— both machines out in the entryway area near my fireplace; the living room where a stereo, its speakers, a TV, and several video recorders were dwarfed by a wall of books— Hammett, Chandler, Cain, Spillane; the tiny green lights on several walls, indicating that key windows and doors in the house were closed, the remnants of a burglar alarm system the former owners had installed, a service I'd let lapse as far as having the alarms tied by phone line to the police was concerned (I explained to her) ever since I'd set them off accidentally three times and was charged fifty bucks per visit by the city; my small cluttered office where my word processor sat on a desk, printer and typewriter on a table, and manuscripts in progress scattered everywhere, the original cover painting for Roscoe Kane's *Murder Me Again, Doll* hanging on the wall facing my work seat.

"You must like those fifties babes," she said wryly, nodding toward the vintage paperback cover painting. Her smile, like the girl in the painting, reminded me of somebody else.

"I guess. But I seem to be living in the eighties."

"Nobody in Port City's living in the eighties."

"Stuck in a time warp, are we?"

"Rod Serling meets you at the city limits," she said, and I led her out of my office, back into the living room, to a sofa that faced the TV/stereo area.

She lit a filtered cigarette, crossed her dark, sleek, unnyloned legs. "Coming back to the Midwest after five years out east was a shock to my system."

"I bet."

She gestured with her cigarette. "It's not so much that Port City's stuck in the fifties or anything. Rather, it's ... timeless, in a creepy midwestern sort of way."

"Now that you've brought the modern wonder called cable to the community, that all should change."

Little laugh. "Have you checked out what's playing on most of the cable channels? Old movies and TV shows. Burns and Allen, Jack Benny, Sgt. Bilko."

And here she hadn't even seen my T-shirt.

"Sure," I said, nodding toward the tube, "and it's the best stuff on."

"True. But when I see those old shows while I'm in Port City, I wonder what year it is. I feel like I could look out the window and Eisenhower would still be president."

"Maybe he is."

She shook her head. "I'm sorry I came back."

"Why *did* you come back?"

Her mouth twitched a smile. "To show people." She looked at me. "Like I said this morning . . . to show you."

I smiled, shrugged. "Consider me shown. I've been kicking myself all day that I didn't take you more seriously back in high school."

She was shaking her head again. "That's the weird thing about it. If you *had* paid attention to me, if you *had* gone with me, if all my dreams *had* come true, and I'd married you and we'd settled down, I wouldn't be who I am."

"You wouldn't."

"Of course not. I wouldn't be this smart, modern woman you're so impressed with. I'd probably be a frumpy housewife with five of your kids. You'd probably have left me by now. We'd probably be divorced."

"I'm surprised we're even speaking."

That got a laugh out of her, and broke the slightly depressing spell she was weaving for herself.

"You know what I mean, though," she said.

"Sure. Maybe I wouldn't have gone to Vietnam. Maybe I wouldn't have traveled around like I did, getting the experience that allowed me to be a writer. And I can't imagine me doing anything else but writing."

She put her cigarette out in the one ashtray I keep on hand for smokers; she kept it with her after that. "So what we're both saying is, we don't really have any regrets."

"I think that's what we're saying. I think we're both glad we are who we are."

Nodding, she said, "We agree it's a good thing we were never an 'item,' back in school."

Nodding, I said, "Best thing that never happened to us."

And she said, "Kiss me. . . ."

"You fool," I said.

And we both laughed.

And both kissed.

And I'll be damned if half an hour later we weren't both embarrassed to be sitting naked next to each other in my bed, having made sweet, tender, enjoyable, and, ultimately, passionate love, more about which I decline to say, only to point out that despite its sweetness, tenderness, enjoyability and passion, we both were incredibly embarrassed about the whole thing, and neither one of us really understood why. Or did I say that already?

"If it was terrific," she said, "why are we both embarrassed?"

"What do you mean, 'if' it was terrific? Didn't you think it was terrific? I thought it was pretty terrific."

"Mal, you were terrific. The earth moved, okay? So why do I feel like shit?"

I touched her arm. "I can't agree."

With a one-handed swing, she hit me with her pillow, in a fairly friendly way, a few embers off the cigarette in her other hand landing on the sheet.

"Okay, okay," I said, flicking away the ashes. "Watch the cigarette, will ya; you'll burn the place down."

"You don't smoke, do you?"

"No."

"Why?"

"I'd rather die some natural way."

"Like getting hit by a bus, you mean?"

"I'm holding out for a heart attack during orgasm at age one hundred five."

"You've always been a wise guy, Mal."

"Are you complaining?"

"No. No, I don't think so."

"Jill. This is very confusing. We're almost fighting now."

"Almost," she said.

I gestured toward the bed and us in it. "If we'd met today, and had tumbled into bed— and I'm not saying either one of us is of loose enough moral character to do such a thing, mind you—but if we had, it wouldn't feel so awkward now. There's four of us in bed, tonight. You and me yesterday, kids; and you and me today, grown-ups."

She put her cigarette out in my one and only ashtray, currently on the nightstand beside her, and rested her head in the hollow of my shoulder.

"There's really five of us in bed," she said.

"Oh?"

"Ginnie's here, too."

She was right. I'd consciously not brought

Ginnie up, wanting to spend the evening with this beautiful young woman from my high school past without that, hoping to get around to one touchy point eventually, but preferring to try to get to know Jill for Jill.

"I talked to Brad Faulkner," I told her.

"What did he have to say?"

I told her all about it; pretty soon she was sitting up in bed, listening too intently to notice, or anyway care, that the sheet was around her waist and her breasts were showing. They weren't large breasts, of the sort this culture worships; rather the sort of nice handfuls that seem to resist gravity despite age beginning to set in. In the flicker of candlelight her dark skin looked too beautiful to be real; *she* looked too beautiful to be real. The nicest part, however, was, she was real.

And I was telling her about Faulkner.

Stunning her, actually.

"Good God," she said, whites of her eyes showing all around the blue. "Who'd have thought it? Brad Faulkner knocked Ginnie up!" Again, she was reverting to high school terminology. "And she had an abortion. God. Must've been pretty rough on her."

"She pretended it wasn't," I said, remembering that night under the stars with Ginnie. "But it was. Why do you suppose she didn't tell him?"

"That's easy," she said, lighting another cigarette, worldly wise. "He'd never've allowed the abortion; he would've married her.

Junior year or not. If the parents wouldn't consent, they'd go out of state."

"And Ginnie didn't want that. She wasn't ready."

"Not a free spirit like Ginnie, Mal, no. And if she'd told Brad about the abortion afterward, he'd have been furious with her. They'd have broken up for good. And he was her Mallory, remember."

"What do you mean?"

A shrug; her breasts bobbed prettily. "The love of her life, high school style." Archly, she added, "Of course, she and Brad obviously consummated *their* love a little sooner than we did. . . ."

"Jill, why did she tell him about that abortion, after all these years?"

"I don't know. I really don't know."

"It was a cruel thing to do, considering the loss of his kid not long ago, his marriage breaking up because of it."

"Mal, we both know Ginnie could be cruel, at short notice."

"You said you'd been having lunch with her, off and on, these past six months. And that the topic of conversation was often 'old times.'"

"That's right. Brad's name came up—but nothing about the abortion. She was looking forward to the reunion, to seeing Brad after all these years."

"Why?"

"She was entertaining fantasies—at least I

thought they were fantasies—of getting back together with him."

"What? I don't believe ..."

"Mal, she was looking for a fresh start. She felt her life was at something of a dead-end, and she was floundering around for something new. She knew Brad was single again, and she made vague reference to his running a business, that hardware store"—she shrugged elaborately—"which may mean she had notions of pooling their collective business acumen in some new venture. Or something."

"But she was way out of Brad Faulkner's league! You can't convince me that Ginnie wanted to come back to Port City and settle down with the likes of Faulkner. And, what— run a hardware store together? Besides—he's a religious fanatic, for Christ's sake. What was she thinking of?"

"You want my opinion?"

"That's why I'm asking."

"I think she'd led a fairly decadent life these last ten or fifteen years. I think she was tired of all that, and had glowing memories of her childhood, including her high school days, and she was fantasizing about returning to Port City and climbing inside a Norman Rockwell painting."

"It never would have worked."

"Of course it wouldn't have. She knew that, too. But it didn't stop her from looking forward to seeing Brad at the reunion."

"But why Brad?"

"I told you! He was her Mallory!"

Her Debbie Lee. I guess I could understand it, after all. Old obsessions are something our brain never quite sorts out of the filing system, never quite discards.

"There's something I should've told you," she said, with an embarrassment that wasn't remotely sexual.

"Which is?"

"That I'm the one who called Brad Faulkner and told him you were asking around about Ginnie."

"I've been trying to think of a nice way to ask you about that."

"I've been trying to think of a nice way to tell you."

"Why'd you do it? Is he a friend of yours or something?"

"No. I just felt I owed it to him, since I gave you his name. Common courtesy. Nothing sinister, Mal. Quit thinking like a mystery writer."

"I am a mystery writer."

"I know. I've read your books."

"No kidding? You're the first person I've met lately who has."

"I didn't say I liked them."

"Thanks a lot."

She grinned. "I *did* like 'em. Even the one that was all about Debbie Lee."

"Debbie Lee. When you mention her, and I remember how stupidly I behaved when she reentered my life, I can believe that Ginnie might honestly have hoped to get something going with Brad Faulkner again. After all these years. At a high school reunion, no less."

"I'll bet that's exactly what she did," Jill said. "I bet she came on to Brad, bubbling about old times, eventually gushing forth some of her dreams about *new* times, and it didn't take. He wasn't having any."

"He *seemed* to be," I said. "They were dancing close at the Elks, hanging all over each other."

"That would've been the 'old times' phase. But after an evening with Ginnie—with who Ginnie had become over these fifteen years—conservative, religious Mr. Faulkner would eventually be turned off. Agreed?"

"Agreed," I said. "And their reunion began turning sour at the Sports Page."

She snapped her fingers, pointed at me. "That's when she got pissed off, and blurted out the abortion story! To hurt him!"

I thought of the cafeteria, years ago, and knew Ginnie was capable of that. Not upon reflection, not with malice aforethought, but with the quick trigger of temper, with the impulse decision of the born risk taker, the gambler, that was Ginnie, all right.

"She would've been sorry later," Jill said. "But she did have it in her to lash out at him that way. If he'd hurt her, disappointed her, crushed her fantasy of him, you can *bet* she'd have opened the closet and let the skeletons come rattling out."

She was right.

"You," I said, "are one of the smartest women I've ever met."

"If you weren't such a sexist boor," she said, smiling, "that would've come out 'smartest persons' you ever met."

"If you're so smart, how come you're in bed with a sexist boor?"

"Ya got me there, Mal. Why's that little green light gone out?"

"Huh?"

"The little green light you told me about. The burglar alarm."

13

I CLUTCHED JILL'S ARM AND WHISPERED: "SOME-body could be in the house."

She breathed my name back, some fear in it; I didn't blame her.

"Just sit tight." I whispered in her ear; hardly a sweet nothing. "Don't make a sound."

I slipped out of bed, my right toes touching my jockey shorts on the floor where I'd discarded them in a considerably more carefree moment. I bent down, found them with my hand, climbed into them, bumping against the chest of drawers as I did. The sound of it was like bumping unwittingly into the car behind you as you parked, but louder. The silence that folowed was louder still.

I felt better with my shorts on—I didn't particularly relish being naked while confronting a midnight intruder—but not that much better. The burglar alarm system I'd inherited covered most of the doors and many of the windows in the house, so I had no real sense of where this possible intruder might have entered. There had been a rash of house break-ins this summer; kids with no jobs looking for loose change and/or kicks. That's probably all this was.

But at the very least a door or a window had been breached. The alarm system had, as I'd told Jill earlier, been disconnected as far as alerting the local cops was concerned and I rarely, almost never, switched the key in the control panel to turn on the loud, neighborhood-rousing alarm that went with the system; that left only the various tiny glowing green lights on walls about the house to provide a constant source of security, telling me my doors and windows were secure.

Or not.

I was in the little connecting nook between my bedroom, study, bathroom, and dining room, the carpet beneath my bare feet helping keep my footsteps down to a minimal squeak. I paused, listening.

I heard nothing.

I edged carefully toward the open door to my study. Listened. Heard nothing. Just my heart pounding.

I moved into the dining room; there was a little light coming from the dining room windows and filtering though sheer curtains:

street light, moonlight, not much, enough to help me and my memory maneuver around chairs, tables and such.

Soon I was in my small kitchen, a little hallway with appliances, the linoleum cold on my soles. Cold on my soul, too. The lingering smell of that Italian sauce I was so proud of now made my stomach turn; why nausea accompanied fear was a puzzle to me—I'd noticed it first in Vietnam, but had never got used to it.

I took tentative steps, because walking made more noise in here; no getting around it. I'd pause between steps, listening, stepping sideways, my back to the stove and dishwasher, brushing their cold metal, so that should anyone enter via the door at either side of the small kitchen, I'd not provide that someone with my back. Also, that allowed me to face the doorway to the basement (here in the kitchen), several windows of which were among those wired to the alarm system, meaning an intruder could be coming up via the basement steps. I crossed to the basement door as silently as I could, shut it as silently as I could, bolted it as silently as I could, which in the latter case meant making the following noise: THUK!, which seemed to echo through the house.

I moved back against the appliances, trembling, waiting, listening.

Nothing.

I began wondering if the alarm system had shut down for some maintenance reason; but every little green light in the system—there were half a dozen of them—couldn't burn out simultaneously. If such were the case, I'd be sure to call Ripley tomorrow. Still, there could be some other bug in the system. Could any intruder be this quiet?

That was when I heard the noise out in the entryway area, a bumping. Unless I missed my guess, someone had just bumped into my pinball machine. Thank you, Bally.

I moved to the kitchen drawers directly across from me, slid one open—it creaked, but just barely—and my hand fell on the tray of silverware within. My hand found the knives alongside the tray—not table-setting knives, not even steak knives, but the carving set a relative had sent last Christmas, a gift I'd never used. I felt for the thickest wooden handle among them, knowing it held the longest, widest blade in the set, and withdrew it, clutching it in my hand like Jim Bowie sitting in his little room at the Alamo, waiting for the Mexican Army to rush in.

There was the faintest squeak of footsteps in the entryway beyond the kitchen—how could anyone learn to walk so quietly? Then a frightening thought came to me: if it was your *job* to walk quietly, you would *learn* how.

This was not some kid, some vandal; this was not just another house break-in. This was, instinct told me, something else. Someone professional. A cop, maybe? If I was lucky, a cop.

Behind me, on the stove, was a light switch; just a small light, a light by the built-in clock on the stove, not enough to illuminate the room, but enough to throw some light on the subject should I feel the need. With my free hand, the one not clutching my carving-set Bowie, I reached for the little switch, rested my fingers on it, and waited.

If he was moving through the house, he would either cut through the bathroom, which with its doors at either end would lead him directly to the bedroom, where Jill waited; or he would come through this kitchen, with the same destination in mind. What little light was filtering in from outside couldn't reach the longer-than-it-was-wide cubbyhole of the kitchen, so I was protected in the darkness. I held my breath. Stood there in my jockey shorts like a side of beef preparing to butcher itself. The knife in my hand, held out to my side, blade up and pointing out slightly, quivering. What a man.

The curtains out in the entryway were open; plenty of light from the street was coming in there—moonlight, too. I could see my neighbor's little bungalow across the street from me with frightening clarity. Then a shape blocked it out.

He was big, rather wide, and had something in his hand.

Something that seemed to be a gun.

Just a silhouette, just a shape, but a shape

to be reckoned with. I had to pee. Thank you, God.

He moved toward the kitchen.

He filled the doorway.

Could he see me? The kitchen was pitch black, what light there was was to his back, I was plastered up against the appliances, but *could he see me?*

No.

He moved right by me; must've stood six-three. He smelled like English Leather. With luck, I smelled like nothing at all. He was approaching the doorway, about to move into the dining room, about three steps away from me, when I hit the little light.

He whirled, a big man in black in a ski mask—hardly the time of year for the latter—and eyes glowed at me, those of a beast caught in headlights on the highway, and the gun in his hand, an automatic with a silencer, just like in the movies, was pointing right at me, and I hurled the knife and it sunk into his shoulder above the arm with the gun in hand and he howled, more like a man than a beast, and the gun pointed down and went *snick*, and chips of linoleum went flying.

He fell backward, pitching into the refrigerator, and I was on him, using the pain in his shoulder to wrest the gun from him. It was in my hand now, and I stood over him, shaking, grinning, saying, "Take the mask off. Christmas is over."

It seemed witty to me at the time.

He sat there, glaring at me—quite an accomplishment, since he was doing it through the circles of the ski mask with just his heavily browed eyes, an oddly attractive shade of green, pretty jewels in ugly settings—and pulled the knife out of his shoulder.

I swallowed.

He pushed himself to his feet.

"Don't do that!" I said. Nothing vaguely witty occurring to me.

He held the knife, blade streaked with his own blood, in his big hand, the hand of the arm ending in the good shoulder, and spoke. His voice was a raspy whisper.

"Give me my gun," he said.

I found myself backing up. I should've shot him on the spot. But I'd never shot anybody in my kitchen before. And I'd never before hurled a knife at somebody and sat him down and seen him get up and take the knife out and lumber toward me, with the grace and, apparently, the pain threshold of Frankenstein's monster.

"I'll shoot," I said. It sounded kind of lame, even to me.

Then he raised the knife in stabbing position and lunged at me, and I shot my refrigerator.

He was on me, a thousand pounds of him was on me, unless I'd killed the Frigidaire and it fell on me, and the gun wasn't in my hand anymore. I had the presence of mind to grab the arm with the knife, with two hands, but the son of a bitch was strong, and then an arm looped around his neck and a hand pulled off his mask, and I got a good look at him being surprised and pissed—green eyes, broken nose, wide mouth, scarred cheekbone —as he must not have known anybody else was in the house.

He stood, tossing Jill off him like a nude little monkey, and she smacked into and rattled against the wounded refrigerator. You would've thought he'd have appreciated having a beautiful naked woman like Jill latch onto him, but no. . . .

Nor did he appreciate me butting him in the nuts; he was tough, but nobody's tough enough to withstand that, and he sat on the floor and clutched his privates, the knife clunking to the linoleum, and I did something I didn't know I ws capable of: I looked quickiy around for and picked up his automatic and smacked him with it, on the side of the head, as hard as I possibly could.

While he was still unconscious, we tied him up with clothesline, called Sheriff Brennan, and put on some clothes. I took time out to pee. Then, waiting for Brennan, I checked the guy's pockets and found no ID. The gun was a nine millimeter Smith and Wesson; the silencer was a round tube with perforations, apparently homemade, but slickly so.

Brennan was there in five minutes, and the guy was still unconscious.

Pushing his Stetson back on his head, kneeling, Brennan touched the guy's head; it was bloody, clotting up. The black shirt around the one shoulder was damp with blood, too.

"Hit him alongside his head a mite hard, wouldn't you say?"

"He shot at me in my goddamn kitchen," I said. "What do you expect me to do?"

Brennan stood, hands on hips, shrugging. "I don't think you killed him."

"You don't think ..." My stomach dropped. "Jesus, I didn't mean ..."

"It ain't like TV," he said solemnly. "Most people don't take blows to the head lightly. I better call a ambulance."

He did.

Jill and I stood in the living room—the big, black-clad intruder was slumped, trussed up in clothesline, on the kitchen floor, his back to the cupboards and drawers, where I'd got the butcher knife. We hugged each other, feeling like we knew each other very well now. Sharing unexpected violence in the night brings people together. The family that slays together stays together.

"Be here in two shakes of a lamb's tail," Brennan said, coming back from the phone. He took the Stetson off, brushed greasy hair off his forehead. "You know that feller?"

"Sure. He lives next door. He wanted a cup of sugar, but he forgot to say please."

Brennan laughed, but not because he thought my limp crack Was anything to laugh about. "You're a pretty tough hombre, ain't ya, Mallory?"

"You got me into this, dammit!"

His face turned serious. I couldn't believe he hadn't made a connection between this and Ginnie Mullens yet.

He said, "You think this has something to do with little Ginnie dyin'?"

"For two days I've been asking around about her, including talking to her drug connection in Iowa City. Then suddenly Arnold Schwartzenegger in a ski mask comes calling at midnight. What do *you* think?"

Brennan thought about it. "He have any ID on him?"

"No."

The sheriff let some air out. "He don't look like a cat burglar at that."

"He's a guy with a gun with a silencer. How do you read it?"

"Like somebody took out a contract."

"Me, too." I glanced at Jill. She had the drawn face of a woman who hadn't slept for days. "Forgive me for thinking like a mystery writer."

"That's okay," she said. "Any time a guy in black comes in your house with a gun with a silencer, you got my permission to think like a mystery writer. By the way, does this sort of thing happen to you often?"

"First time this week," I said. "Brennan, this guy is obviously not local."

He nodded. "This kind of thing *can* be set up in these parts. There are bars in South End where you can set up a hit for a hundred dollars."

"That's a generous estimate," I said, thinking of certain bars in that part of town. "But I don't think this is a hundred-dollar contract."

"Me neither," Brennan admitted.

The wail of an ambulance interrupted us, and soon we were untying our slumbering charge and he was being loaded onto a stretcher; Brennan kept a gun on the slack figure in case he was "playin' possum." He sent a deputy along in the ambulance, and stayed behind with me.

We stood in front of my house. On the corner across from me, there is no house, simply a bluff, way down at the bottom of which is the Mississippi, which I can see from my place. A nearly full moon was shimmering on the river, rippling there. The winking amber lights of barges, having just come through the lock and dam, multiplied themselves in reflections on the water.

Jill went back inside to put herself together, while Brennan and I stood looking across the street toward that bluff where the river and the trees beyond it formed the horizon.

He said, "I didn't mean to get you in anything this deep."

"This was nothing either one of us could predict."

"Maybe you ought to stop. Maybe we ought to sit down tomorrow, and you fill me in on what you've got, and just call it a day. I'll do my best to take 'er from there."

"I appreciate that, Sheriff. But I better see this through."

I don't believe what he said next, because he said it without a trace of humor.

"Well," he yawned, "a man's gotta do what a man's gotta do."

I just looked at him.

He gave me a slip of paper. "Address of Ginnie's hippie husband, up in the Cities. Case you want to talk at him."

In spite of what I'd been through, I found a grin. "Much obliged, Sheriff," I said.

He tipped his Stetson, said, "Keep outa trouble," and drove off, siren silent.

Inside, I turned the burglar alarm system on, including the loud alarm I usually left off.

Jill was waiting.

She was in bed. She was naked.

And, no longer strangers, we made love, with a slow, yearning quality that came out of a heightened awareness of our mortality.

We didn't even turn out the lights.

And we weren't embarrassed at all—before, during, or after.

14

THE NEXT MORNING I WAS DRIVING ON HIGH-
way 61, squinting into a bright sun; me, I
didn't feel so bright. Jill had left early,
barely after sunup, to go home and shower
and get ready for work; she seemed more
shaken, more troubled this morning than she
had in the thick of things last night. Holding
each other in the dark had made getting
through the early morning hours a snap;
getting through the day on our own would
be a whole 'nother deal.

I hadn't been able to get back to sleep
after Jill left, so at nine o'clock I was sitting
at the Sports Page having breakfast—biscuits
and gravy, very good but settling in my
stomach like an anchor. Shortly after I was
on the road. I felt a little stiff from my

skirmish with the guy in my kitchen last night, and a little uneasy about the direction my unofficial investigation into Ginnie's death was taking. Specifically, that direction was (at the moment anyway) the Quad Cities, which despite its name included half a dozen cities and a handful or smaller municipalities, about a half-million population's worth sprawled along either side of the Mississippi River as it separated Iowa from Illinois.

Ginnie's husband, J.T. O'Hara, whose absence at his wife's funeral had puzzled me, managed a used-book store atop Harrison Street hill in Davenport, on the Iowa side of the Quad Cities. Because Harrison is a one-way falling downhill toward the river, I had to travel the uphill one-way of Brady, and circle around. Once I'd parked, I felt as though I'd stepped not from my car but out of a time machine taking me into 1969.

The Used Book Exchange was on a commercial strip that seemed, for a couple blocks anyway, to be a hippie ghetto. The shop was stuck between a co-op health-food grocery store whose window bragged about its prices on tofu and sprouts, and a restaurant seeking to pull hungry folks off the street with the lure of soyburgers. Just across the way was a used-record store cum head shop, next to which was a seedy-looking new-wave/punk bar advertising its next band via graffiti in its own window: *The Reaganomics*, the band seemed to be called. The Exchange itself was like a dining car, one end of which was stuck rudely toward the street, a narrow storefront with brightly colorful big letters spelling out its name in the window; smaller, the words MOVIE POSTERS and USED COMICS were also spelled out, and some comic books were propped up in the window underground comics (*Zap, Freak Bros., Mr. Natural*) mingling with superheroes (*X-Men, Batman, Fantastic Four*); all were sixties vintage. The shop opened at ten, and it was just after that now, so the OPEN sign was turned my way in the door. In I went.

The shop's interior was deep, a surprisingly tidy room where a wall of books on either side faced several aisles of bookcases that stood taller than me; paperbacks mostly. Just inside the door, to my left as I came in, was a squared off counter, a little newsstand-like structure, behind which a skinny, balding, bearded man sat on a stool by the cash register reading a magazine called *Denver Quarterly*.

Despite its being summer, the man wore a green lint-flecked sweater; of course—an ancient air conditioner chugged in a port in the window behind him, and it was fairly chilly up in the front of the narrow shop. Hanging from thumbtacks at just above eye level from a wooden strip atop the newsstand-like counter were comic books from the fifties: *Superman, Little Lulu* and, I was pleased to note, *Sgt. Bilko* (half a dozen boxes of old comics stood on the floor in front of the counter). Also hanging from thumbtacks were 8-by-10-inch glossies of movie stars, ranging from Clint Eastwood to Clark Gable, from Woody Allen to the Three Stooges. A sign advised that movie posters were available; just ask—and various posters were taped to the ceiling—*Superman*, *Return of the Jedi*, *Indiana Jones and the Temple of Who Cares*. No blown-up covers of *Denver Quarterly*.

J.T. O'Hara nodded at me (I was in a black T-shirt and jeans today), smiled, said, "Let me know if you need some help," and went back to reading his literary magazine, not recognizing me.

I browsed for a while. The place was very orderly, broken into sections, with historical romance and Harlequin romances and other women's paperback pulp dominating; the mystery section was in the back, and I found a copy of one of my books there, personally inscribed to somebody at some book-signing I'd done—glad to see my personal touch had meant so much. I also found a couple first printings of Mickey Spillane and Roscoe Kane paperbacks, picked 'em up. Everything within a given section was in alphabetical order; O'Hara was doing a good job with the little shop—it was hardly the jumble many such paperback exchange shops are—and his hippie roots were only showing here and there, such as in the extremely left-wing political section. Those roots were especially showing in the poetry section, where prominently displayed among Yeats and McKuen were several chapbooks by J.T. O'Hara, published by Toothpaste Press of West Branch, Iowa. The newest was entitled *A Shroud for Aquarius*. I thumbed through the little book, found the title poem, next to a grainy sepia photograph of a sun going down, or maybe coming up.

> *Find tie-dye linen*
> *To lay her to rest*
> *Shed paisley tears*
> *Aquarius sets*

That almost rhymed, but I wasn't sure if it was supposed to. I didn't know whether it was a good poem or not (though I might venture a guess: not) but at least I could tell what it was about.

I carried a copy of *A Shroud for Aquarius* up to the counter, along with my Spillane and Kane, dug six bucks out of my billfold; the sale of his own book perked J.T. O'Hara up. So did the odd literary company I'd placed him in, I think. He put the literary magazine he'd been reading face down on the counter, fanned open to where his place was.

"Mickey Spillane and I seldom find the same readers," he said, slate eyes coming alive, sliding the books into a used paper bag, "but I salute your catholic taste." He was my age though his crow's feet were deeper. It's not that I look young for my age—it's just that he didn't. The full but carefully tended beard could not hide deep lines, and gray freely mingled with the brown of his hair and beard. He was an old hippie, all right, but he did not have the drugged-out, burnt-out look in his eyes that normally characterizes the breed.

"I found the title poem very interesting," I said.

"Really? Not much of a poem. Something I scribbled off."

"Why would you name the volume after what you see as one of your lesser poems?"

He shrugged; he was my size but skinnier, and looked frail—shrugging seemed a risk. "The editor at Toothpaste Press suggested the title for the collection. Said it summed up what all the poems in the volume are about."

"The end of the sixties, you mean."

His eyes brightened further. "Right. The dreams that didn't come true. The idealism that turned to ash."

"Those were the good old days, by your way of thinking."

"Sure! Never better. Something was in the air."

"Yeah," I said. "Pot smoke."

"Mallory," he said, standing. Eyes narrowing. "I didn't recognize you at first."

"What gave me away, finally?"

"The cynicism. You're here to talk about Ginnie, I suppose."

"Yes I am. I'm surprised you recognized me at all. We only met a couple of times."

"Ginnie spoke of you often. You were her best friend, growing up."

"I always thought of her as my best friend," I admitted. "It's nice to hear that she felt the same about me."

"You really loved Ginnie, didn't you?"

He meant "loved" in the sixties sense; he knew there'd never been anything romantic between us.

"Yes I did," I said. "Even though we drifted apart."

He smiled; his teeth looked a little bad. "Not everybody was able to love Ginnie. She had her faults."

"She had a tongue like a knife," I said.

"You're a poet yourself," J.T. said, "albeit of the Raymond Chandler school. My memories of Ginnie's tongue conjure rather more lyrical images than a blade. But I'll grant you her temper could slash you."

"Did her temper ever slash *you*?"

He risked another shrug. "From time to time. The sort of wounds that don't ever heal completely; but neither do they debilitate."

"Why did you live apart?"

"Why did we live together?"

"Because you loved each other?"

"A reasonable assumption."

"J.T.," I said, "we're alone here. There's no one else in the store. You don't have to talk in circles. Life isn't a poem."

"But it is poetic."

"Justice is, sometimes—not life. If you still loved Ginnie, and she still loved you, why didn't you stay together? When did you split, exactly?"

He sat back down. "Two years ago."

"Why?"

"I loved her too much to be a part of it."

"A part of what?"

"Her life. And I didn't want Mal to be part of it, either."

He meant their four-year-old daughter, Malinda; I knew that was what he meant almost at once, but hearing the name attached to Ginnie's child jarred me, just the same.

"You didn't want ... Mal to be part of Ginnie's life ... in what *way*, J.T.? The gambling? The crazy trips to Vegas and Tahoe?"

"No. I didn't like that much, but she was her own person, she could do as she liked."

"What bothered you about Ginnie's lifestyle, then? What was it that a free spirit like you couldn't handle in a free spirit like her?"

"I don't think I care to talk about it."

"What if I told you Ginnie may have been murdered."

He flinched, then smiled—not a convincing smile, but a smile. "Life isn't a mystery novel."

"I disagree."

"A mystery, yes. A mystery novel, no." The smile curled into a sneer, emphasized by the mustache of his beard. "I don't remember liking you much, Mallory. Your cynicism always rubbed me the wrong way. Out of respect to Ginnie's love for you, I won't throw you out bodily, but will just ask you to go."

This guy could not throw a puppy out of this place bodily. Putting on my best cynical smart-ass smile, I leaned on the counter with one hand, with the other giving him the peace sign; he gave me half of the peace sign in return.

I ignored that. Said, "Was Ginnie involved with drugs? Is that why you didn't want your little girl around her?"

"Just go, Mallory."

"Talk to me, J.T. Help me find out why Ginnie is dead."

He slammed a fist down on the counter; the *Denver Quarterly* jumped. So did I. I didn't expect this power from such a frail-looking man, or this rage from so laid back a source.

"She's dead," he said, spitting words like seeds, "because that time is dead, because those days are over."

I laughed at that, though without much humor. "She isn't dead just because the *sixties* are dead. She's not an image in one of your poems, or a symbol in one of my novels, either. She's a person who was murdered, shot in the goddamn head, J.T.! And I want to find out who did that so the state can serve up some old-fashioned justice, poetic or otherwise."

He swallowed. "Can I get you some tea?"

"Sure."

"What kind?"

"The kind you don't smoke."

He smiled at that, just a little, and put a kettle of water on the hotplate that rested on the chugging air conditioner. He dropped in a tea bag. He turned and looked at me; his gray eyes seemed very, very old.

"She was involved in drugs, all right," he said. "But not in using them. Not to any excessive extent, anyway."

"Dealing, then?"

"No. Not exactly."

"What, then?"

He paused. Thought. Then, as if against his better judgment, said, "She was working for a guy named Sturms. You know him?"

"I know him."

"She was his mule. One of them."

"Mule."

"You know. She'd go to Mexico, ostensibly on buying trips for her shop, picking up furniture and knickknacks for ETC.'s . . ."

"Among which were hidden quantities of coke and other illegal goodies?"

He sighed. Nodded.

"Yeah. I figured that's what Caroline Westin wanted to put a stop to."

"What?"

"Her partner in ETC.'s, Caroline Westin, recently squeezed her out of the business—you knew that, didn't you, J.T.?"

He shrugged again; he didn't seem so frail to me now. Bony, yes—frail, no. "I knew Ginnie got bought out of ETC.'s," he said, "but assumed it happened because she wanted it to. I didn't know Caroline forced her out, to put a stop to the shop being involved in drug trafficking. But it makes sense. Caroline was pretty bitter about Ginnie getting back together with me. You see—and I hope this doesn't bruise your sensibilities, Mallory, since like most cynics you're naive at heart, but . . ."

"Caroline and Ginnie were lovers," I cut in. "Yeah. And Ginnie broke off with her to marry you."

"Yes. Well. To get together with me."

"I thought you were married."

Another shrug. He was pouring us some tea now, in unmatching, chipped china cups. "Sort of. We never had a ceremony. We were together long enough to rate common law, I suppose."

I took the cup of tea and sipped; orange. "So that's why she didn't take your last name."

"She probably wouldn't have even if we *had* married. She was just . . . well, she was using me, in a way," he said.

"Ginnie did do that with people from time to time. How did she use *you*?"

He spooned some honey into his tea cup; stirred. "She wanted a child. It was something she wanted to experience." He laughed; in that laughter was the first trace of bitterness in him about Ginnie. "Then once she'd had the little girl, she lost interest." He looked at me sharply. "I'm not saying she didn't love Malinda. I'm not saying she was a bad mother, either."

"It's just that she dropped the baby off at a day-care center on the way home from the hospital, right?"

"No! Not at all. She was a very good mother, those early months. She breast-fed Malinda, for one thing. Would a bad mother breast-feed her child?"

"I guess not. What happened after the early months?"

He did't look at me; he looked into his tea, stirring it absently. "She went back to work, back to ETC.'s. I stayed home. That was fine—she was bringing the money in. I've been publishing my poetry right along, but half the time I get paid off in contributor's copies. When I do get money, it isn't much. Twenty-five bucks from the *Iowa Review* twice a year doesn't buy many groceries."

"Hey," I said. "I'm a free-lancer myself. You don't have to apologize."

"I'm *not* apologizing! I was a house husband. I'm proud of it. I did a good job. Why should I apologize? John Lennon didn't!" He set his cup down and splashed some tea on the *Denver Quarterly*.

"Settle down, J.T. I'm on your side, on this one."

He studied me, saw that I was. Said, "Ginnie loved our little girl. She just wasn't much of a traditional mother. And, to her credit, when I told her I was leaving, that I wouldn't be party to the drug traffic, that I wouldn't have my daughter raised around it, she didn't fight me over Malinda. She let me take her with me."

"Maybe she knew who the better parent was."

"Maybe," he said, not disputing it. "But she did love Mal. Malinda. She'd take her for the weekend once every month or so. Show her a wonderful time. They used to go to Adventureland Park at Des Moines, for example."

"Ginnie was nothing if not adventurous."

"Unfortunately," he agreed.

"Who's taking care of Malinda now?"

He pointed upstairs. "I'm living with a wonderful woman, who is also a poet. She helps me run this place, and we take turns spending time with Malinda."

"You're doing a nice job here."

"Thanks. The movie and comic book stuff helps. There are more Three Stooges buffs around here than Robert Frost fans."

"If you ask me, Shemp was a major poet."

He smiled again, a smile so faint it almost got lost in the nest of his beard. "Why are you doing this?"

"Doing what?"

"Looking into Ginnie's death. If she *was* murdered, you're treading dangerous water. That guy Sturms is connected."

By "connected," he meant organized-crime connected.

"Nobody who deals coke on a major level isn't connected," I said.

The subject seemed one he wanted to change. "Would you like to meet Malinda?" he asked.

"I sure would," I said, smiling.

He picked up the phone and dialed, sipping his tea for the first time. "Hi, babe. Old friend of mine dropped by ... bring Mal down. I'd like her to meet him."

The sound of footsteps clomped on stairs, a door opened in a wall at left that was otherwise a bookcase and a woman and a child entered. The plain, pigtailed, a-few-months pregnant woman in a blue sundress, over the top of which her pale bosom was blossoming, held the hand of a pretty little girl of about four, long red hair cascading onto the shoulders of a Strawberry Shortcake T-shirt. Her pants were pink and a little worn, probably secondhand, and she wore sandals. She had the memory of jam on her face, and looked like an urchin—but a well-fed, happy one. The face was Ginnie's, mostly, the blue eyes particularly.

I went to the little girl and smiled at her. She wasn't shy at all; she looked up and grinned right at me, saying, "Hi."

"Hi," I said, bending down to her level, looking her right in her mother's eyes.

"My name's Malinda. Everybody calls me Mal."

"Everybody calls me Mal, too."

"Really? But you're a boy."

"It's the kind of name that both boys and girls can use."

That seemed to go right by her; she just smiled at me with the bright yet empty eyes of childhood.

I said, "I was a friend of your mommy's."

"Mommy's on a trip."

I hadn't realized they hadn't told the little girl yet.

"I start preschool this year," she said.

"Good for you."

"Are you going to see Mommy?"

"I don't know, honey. . . ."

"If you see Mommy, say hi."

"Okay. I will."

She tugged at the pregnant woman's hand, looking at me as she said, "We're going next door for granola bars. Wanna come?"

"No, thanks," I said, standing. "It was nice meeting you."

They were out the door; the woman and I were never introduced, but exchanged a smile through the storefront window as the girl herded her along.

"I haven't found a way to tell her," he Said.

"You ought to."

"She's so little."

"She's four going on fourteen. Tell her."

"I suppose I should."

"Is that why you weren't at the funeral?"

He sighed heavily. "I called Ginnie's mother. Originally we were going to be there, but I backed out. Said Malinda had a cold."

"It isn't an easy thing to face, is it?"

"No. I loved Ginnie. I still do. But she was still living her life only for herself, for her whims, one gamble after another. She never . . . never really lived up to the responsibilities of being a grown-up."

"That's a problem for a lot of people our age. Those good old days of yours were a supremely selfish time, despite all the love-generation talk. We were a bunch of spoiled kids, rebelling against those who gave us everything."

He looked at me sadly. "Is that how you see the sixties?"

"Sometimes. Hell, what else were we, but spoiled brats who thought we discovered politics, when all we really discovered was dope."

"I smoke a little dope still," he said, reflectively, sipping his tea, "but that's about the extent of my . . . chemical recreation these days. I was part of the drug culture, but I'm not proud of it. Not proud of the way it's hung onto our generation, and spilled over into the next and the next . . . I don't let my daughter see me smoke dope. I don't know, maybe I'm being hypocritical in that."

"Don't sweat it," I said. "She'll probably see her friends doing it when she's in grade school."

That prospect didn't cheer him up.

"Maybe Aquarius isn't dead yet," he said.

"Maybe it should be," I said.

I finished my tea, picked up the paper bag of books, told him he had a nice daughter, and left.

15

THE PORT CITY JAIL WAS ACROSS FROM THE courthouse, the latter a big white stone wedding cake of a structure that had an entire city block to itself and its sloping-on-all-sides lawn. The jail was considerably less grandiose, taking up only half a block, the rest of which was given over to a more modern, sprawling, one-story building that had once been a supermarket but which now housed a mental health clinic and the driver's license bureau—any connection between which I'll leave for you to draw. As for the jail, it resembled nothing more than a rather ordinary stone cottage, if a tad oversize. Of course most ordinary stone cottages don't have three stories, a back yard enclosed by a ten-foot electrical fence, and windows with iron bars barely visible through thick wire-mesh cages. Anyone next door in search of either better mental health or a driver's license might view this barred, wired, electric cottage as an incentive to drive the straight and narrow.

I parked out front, fed the meter (I too was driving the straight and narrow) and walked up the steps and inside, into the outer office, a room as wide as the building but not very deep. Paneled in light pine, its walls were decorated with framed documents and the complimentary calendars of several local businesses; there were four files, three desks, two vending machines (milk, coffee, Pepsi) and one deputy. It was still the lunch hour. I nodded to the deputy—who was younger than me, always a disconcerting thought—and he nodded toward Brennan's office, indicating the sheriff was expecting me. I walked between two desks down a narrow hall and knocked at the door at its dead-end.

"Come on in," Brennan's voice said.

He was sitting behind his desk, studying a computer printout. His Stetson and summer-jacket were on a coat rack to my left as I came in; the pine-paneled office was small, the desk and Brennan's comfy chair and a few spare uncomfy chairs the only furniture. On the wall to the right were three pictures, each of ducks in flight, coordinated so that the ducks seemed to be trying to fly out of one picture into the next, leaving the final duck with nowhere to go. On the wall to the left were framed clippings of a big murder case about fifteen years ago that Brennan had cracked: a local woman stabbed her husband with a pair of scissors and, thanks to an infamous local legal whiz, got off with a year, and has been serving meals around the corner at her Katie's Snack Kitchen ever since. The wall behind Brennan bore no pictures or clippings, just a window with a view, the view being iron bars, wire cage.

Brennan looked unhappy, even a little disgusted. He motioned toward one of the spare chairs, and I pulled it up and sat. He studied the read-out, saying, "Your friend's name is Novack. James C. Novack."

"My friend?"

He looked up, aimed some of his disgust my way. "The feller that dropped by your place around midnight, to rassle?"

"Oh. He's still in the hospital, I suppose."

"Nope. They let him out for the arraignment."

I leaned forward. "When the hell was that?"

"This morning. Bail was set at ten grand."

"Bail! He tried to *kill* me...."

"No," Brennan said, waving a finger at me. "Simple B and E, possible A and B."

"He had a gun! That makes it at *least* ADW—"

"No," Brennan said calmly—a fake calm. "He didn't fire it at you. You were the only guy that fired it."

I smacked a fist in a palm, both of which

were my own. "I should've been at that arraignment."

Brennan shrugged elaborately. "You weren't required to be; you weren't needed, neither. Your statement was on record. It wasn't no trial."

"But there will *be* a trial, won't there?"

A less elaborate shrug. "Maybe. He made bail."

"Shit!"

"Luther Cross was representing him."

Cross was that aforementioned infamous local legal whiz; sixty-some sharp-witted years of age now, Cross was a sleaze in a three-piece suit, the town's most notorious slumlord as well as the guy to call if you killed somebody with a pair of scissors.

"Back in the forties," Brennan said nostalgically, "they say Cross was tied in with the Chicago crowd."

"Legends," I said dismissively.

Local legends had the Chicago mob connected to Port City elements as far back as the twenties and thirties, bootlegging days, up through the late fifties, when a reform mayor cleaned out several notorious blocks in town where gambling and prostitution flourished. Meredith Wilson did not have Port City in mind when he wrote *The Music Man*.

"Really?" Brennan said. "Would you like to know who James C. Novack is?"

"Sure."

"He has a couple dozen assault charges, no

convictions, four murder charges, no convictions, and ... well, let's just say he has no known convictions, and leave 'er at that."

I swallowed. "Where's he from?"

"I'll give you a hint. They got a lake, and they got some wind."

"Shit."

He prodded the readout with a forefinger. "What we suspected last night seems to be the case ... Novack wasn't no house-breaker. He was there to kill you."

I couldn't find anything to say to that at first; the silence in the little room was, to coin a phrase, deafening.

Finally I managed a smile and said, "A Chicago hitman, in Port City, Iowa. How can you expect me to buy that?"

Brennan's Marlboro man mug creased in a wide smile. "You don't have to buy it. Somebody else bought it. It's free, far as you're concerned."

"And the son of a bitch is out on bail."

"Right. But I'd guess he's probably on his way back to Chicago by now."

"You think he'll show up for the trial?"

Brennan gave me a facial shrug. "It's a crap shoot. He might skip—or he might come back 'n' face the music. If he does, he won't get much of a sentence—might pay him and who hired 'im to sit it out in stir."

"I don't believe this."

"I *would*, were I you, young man."

I rubbed the sweat off my face; it was air-conditioned in here, but I was sweating.

So would you, in my shoes. "I don't feel much like a young man anymore, Brennan."

"You want to move in with me, for a spell?"

That startled me.

"Don't scrape the bottom of your jaw on my desk," he said, trying to sound gruff. "It's an honest offer, take 'er if you like, or not."

He lived upstairs, the whole upper floor was his living quarters, the nicest apartment with bars on the windows in town; I'd been there many times, when I was a high school kid, hanging out with his son John. Whose picture was on the desk facing Brennan right this minute.

"I may take you up on that," I said. "I sure do appreciate the offer anyway."

He shrugged, and somebody knocked on his door.

"Come on in," Brennan said.

The silver-mirrored shades of Detective Evans of the Iowa City P.D. peeked in. "Mind if I join the party, gents? Just happened to be in the neighborhood. . . ."

Brennan waved him in. Evans whipped off the sunglasses, stuck them behind the black beeper in the pocket of his white shirt, the sleeves of which were rolled to the elbow. He was again in jeans with the big turquoise belt buckle, and he pulled up a chair, flashed me his dazzler of a smile, looking blindingly white in that dark, mustached face of his, sat with one ankle on the opposite knee, showing off his new tooled leather cowboy boots, and said, "You're in a heap of trouble, boy."

I sighed. "Very funny."

"Not really," Evans admitted. "I never met a Chicago hitman. What's it like?"

"The Vietcong, only taller."

Evans considered that, smiling again, but keeping his teeth to himself. "My guess is this one's tied in with Sturms."

"Safe guess," I said.

Brennan said, "Why don't you fill us both in, Mallory, on the people you been talkin' to. Then we'll fill you in, some."

"Well," I said. "I can start off by saying there's no shortage of suspects, where building a case for Ginnie being murdered is concerned. She was a wonderful person in many respects—and a not so wonderful person in a lot of others."

And I told them most of what I'd found out.

That ex-Yippie propaganda minister, current flack-for-hire Dave Flater, had broken up bitterly with Ginnie, that Ginnie owed him ten grand, that they'd argued violently in front of his receptionist.

That Caroline Westin, Ginnie's partner in ETC.'s, had also been at one time her lesbian lover (Brennan almost swallowed his tongue on that one) and their business dealings of late had been bitter indeed.

That Ginnie's blubbery brother Roger had hardly been blubbering over his sister's death at the funeral home, in fact couldn't have been colder, and admitted having had "words" with Ginnie hours before her death, when she refused to finance his latest computer pipe dream.

That Ginnie had recently revealed to Brad Faulkner, her already emotionally distraught, straight-laced former boyfriend, that she had, back in high school days, aborted his child without even telling him she was pregnant.

"Classy lady," Evans said.

"In many ways she was," I said. "But I can't defend her every act. I can only say she was a complex, intelligent, flawed human being."

"Have you left anything out?" Brennan asked, trying to look eagle-eyed, coming off bug-eyed.

"Isn't that enough?" I said.

Actually, I had left out one item: that Ginnie and Jill Forest had argued at the reunion. But that seemed minor, and Jill had no apparent motive, so I kept it to myself.

"What about this guy Sturms?" Brennan wanted to know.

"She was his mule. That came as no real surprise to me—I knew she'd been that at one time, and it was looking like she'd been smuggling dope for him right along—" I glanced at Evans. "—despite her assurances to the Iowa City Chamber of Commerce to the contrary."

"Sturms is the Chicago connection," Evans said, "obviously."

"Right," I said. "But that doesn't make

him anything special as a possible murder suspect. My snooping around in this thing— poking into Ginnie's drug connections—that's enough right there to get the likes of Novack set loose on me."

Both men nodded.

Evans was stroking his mustache thoughtfully. "You don't see Sturms as a prime suspect, then? Assuming Ginnie Mullens was murdered."

I held my palms up. "Where's the motive? Everybody and his dog's got a motive. Everybody else but *Sturms*, that is. Why would Sturms kill his loyal mule?"

"Mules, dogs," Brennan said, scowling, "forget that crap: it's the *human* animal we're concerned with here."

"That sounds real profound, Brennan," I said, "but I'll be damned if it makes any sense to me."

He shook his finger at me, not in anger. "Sturms is the key. Tell him, Ev."

I looked at Evans and Evans looked at me.

He said, "I got a call this morning from the A-1 Detective Agency in Chicago."

Brennan was nodding. "So did I," he said, gravely.

"Never heard of 'em," I said.

"It's a major firm," Evans said. "Anyway, they're representing Life-Investors Mutual. They'll be sending a man in to investigate, probably tomorrow."

"Life-Investors Mutual?" I said, puzzled. "What's their interest in this?"

Ev smiled on one side of his face. "Your friend Ginnie Mullens bought some insurance from them. Life insurance. Half a million worth. Of course, that's double indemnity, in case of accidental death—which includes murder. Meaning . . ."

"If somebody did murder Ginnie," I said, "Life-Investors Mutual has to cough up . . . good God."

Brennan was nodding.

"A million dollars," he said.

16

THAT AFTERNOON I FOUND MYSELF DRIVING
along Highway 22, careful not to get picked
up in West Liberty's fabled speed trap, glid-
ing through Grant Wood country, turning off
onto the blacktop that led to Ginnie's farmhouse. The green rolling hills conspired with
the pavement to reflect the bright July sun
back at me; once I reached for my sunglasses, only to realize I was already wearing
them. Corn was growing. Cattle grazed. All
was life. Even the sight of the farmhouse
where Ginnie died couldn't dim this day.

Brennan had given me a key—the place
wasn't sealed off as a crime scene, but the
sheriff had retained a key until at least after
the inquest—but the door was unlocked. The
air-conditioning hit me full blast, and at

once I saw, in the high-ceilinged living room
with its earth tones and antiques and plants,
Ginnie's mother—wearing a pink and blue
floral housedress, her hair in curlers under a
red scarf—on her knees boxing things up. At
the moment the lava lamp, which she looked
at uncomprehendingly, was joining several
art deco statues in a cardboard home.

"Excuse me, Mrs. Mullens," I said. "I
didn't see your car. . . ."

Mal!" she said. She rose, put the box
down, and crossed the living room, a pudgy
little woman navigating around half a dozen
already packed boxes, to greet me. "What a
pleasant surprise. You just missed Roger."

"That's a shame."

"He just took the car into West Liberty to
get some groceries," she said, pointing in the
general direction of the little town. No liquor
on her breath today. "We're going to be here
awhile, packing up Ginnie's things."

"I see."

She sighed, took off her wire glasses and
rubbed her eyes. "It's been a long day."

She did look weary.

I said, "Have you been at this long?"

"Just a few hours, actually. We'll be selling
the house, but first we have to sort through
personal items and dispose of the furnishings
and such."

"You're planning a yard sale, then?"

Another sigh. "Eventually. We haven't had
the reading of the will yet, but Mr. Cross told

me confidentially that Ginnie had left everything to us. Roger and me."

"Really?" So the ubiquitous Luther Cross had been Ginnie's attorney; interesting.

She beamed at me. "Seems she loved us, after all."

"It would seem so."

"Oh, apparently there are a few personal knickknacks earmarked for a few other relatives and friends." She frowned. "Hardly seems right that she didn't leave anything to her daughter, but Ginnie had her own way of looking at things, her own way of doing things." She touched my arm. "Don't think me terrible—but this means so much to me. Being remembered by Ginnie like this. As for her daughter, little Malinda, well—anything Ginnie left me, I'm putting it in *my* will for her. It'll be something she'll have to fall back on when she's older."

Mrs. Mullens meant well, but seeing as she was preparing to sell everything in the house, before the flowers on Ginnie's grave had had a chance to wilt, and the house itself shortly after, I didn't figure there'd be much left to pass along to Malinda when the time came. Her son Roger would see to that—the loving brother whose idea this obviously was, this quick sale of everything that wasn't nailed down, after which everything nailed down would also be sold, I had little doubt.

"Don't think ill of me," she said, painfully earnest. Her joy seemed diluted by a drop or so of shame.

"I won't," I assured her, taking her hand, pressing it. "I'd like to take a look upstairs. Do you mind?"

"Go right ahead." She glanced up the plant-lined staircase, shuddered. "I ... I haven't been able to go up there yet."

I touched her shoulder, smiled, and started up. She returned to the living room and her boxes. I wondered how fast the coke mirrors would go at the yard sale.

I entered the small, book-lined room where Ginnie died. Glanced at the familiar titles and authors—James M. Cain, Willard Motley, so many others I'd turned her onto, and others that had turned her on—Tim Leary, Castaneda and crew. And the shelf of gambling books, Goren and company.

I sat at the rolltop desk where she'd died. Sun streamed through the window, finding its way around the leaves of a tree just outside; the smear on the pane had been cleaned off, but the bullet hole in the wood was still there, enlarged a bit—the bullet itself having been dug out by Brennan's crack deputies, no doubt. The scattered papers, now matted and crusty black with her blood, were still where I'd seen them that first night. They had not been gathered as evidence. The brass burner with the engraved Indian designs also hadn't been moved; that half-smoked joint was gone—one of the deputies probably finished it. But little since the other night was changed. Only the smell of incense failed to linger. The sun streaming in through leaves and window seemed only to obscure things—casting pools of light, making meaningless patterns upon those blood-spattered papers.

I was still thinking about the conversation with Brennan and Evans; it hadn't ended with the revelation of Ginnie's million-dollar insurance policy.

There had been other revelations.

"Who's the beneficiary?" I'd asked.

"The little girl," Brennan said. "She lives with her old man. Didn't you go up to the Cities and see him today?"

"Yes," I said. "Just came from there."

Evans grunted. "Better add him to your list of suspects."

"Huh?"

"If his daughter stands to make a million via her mom's murder, I'd say that makes the father a prime suspect."

I gave him as foul a look as I could muster. "Why don't you add the daughter to the list? Four-year-olds these days are a pretty cold-blooded breed, I hear."

"Where was she the night her momma died?" Evans asked, only half kidding.

"Me," I said, "I'm wondering if there's some connection with Dave Flater—he's the P.R. man for Investors Mutual, you know."

"Probably a coincidence," Evans said, shrugging it off. Then he sat forward and gestured with a forefinger. "But I got something else that might not be."

"Oh?"

"Sturms," Evans said.

"Sturms," Brennan said.

"Sturms," I said. "So?"

"So," Evans said, "Sturms was the insurance agent who sold Ginnie the policy. Actually, several policies, adding up to a million, should double indemnity be invoked."

I'd almost forgotten Sturms ran an insurance agency as a front for his coke action.

I said, "What do you make of that?"

Evans shrugged again. "I'm not sure. But keep in mind the Investors Mutual policies don't pay on suicide."

"Maybe Sturms killed her," Brennan offered, "to get a piece of the million-dollar payoff."

Evans shook his head. "Doubtful. He'd have to be in league with the little girl's father, that hippie poet—and besides, if Ginnie Mullens *was* murdered, whoever did it faked it up as a *suicide.* Meaning, do not pass go, do not collect a million dollars. Or a half million, either."

Brennan kept trying. "That shows Sturms probably *did* kill her—faking the suicide, since murder would mean the policies he sold her *would* pay out!"

I was shaking my head, now. "But *why* would he kill her? What's his motive?"

Nobody had an answer to that.

Including me. Sitting here at Ginnie's desk, no answers came to me either. I needed to find some soon; in a day or two, some hotshot investigator from the A-1 Detective

Agency of Chicago would be here running circles around me (and Brennan and Evans), working to prove suicide and save Investors Mutual a million dollars. On the other hand, if I could show this was indeed murder, that sweet little urchin I'd met today, the little red-headed four-year-old in the Strawberry Shortcake T-shirt, the little girl who'd sort of been named after me, would have a rosy financial future indeed. The prospect of which pleased me.

And what did I do about it? I sat staring at the pattern the sun filtering through the leaves coming in the window made on the blood-spattered papers.

Absently, I spread the papers out, like a hand of poker. If it *had* been suicide, why didn't she leave a note? After all, she'd apparently been sitting here in the nude on a hot summer night shortly before her death, doodling, figuring. "Arithmetic," Brennan had called it that night. A few columns of addition; some multiplication.

A worm crawled into my brain and started wriggling.

I sat up; studied the papers more closely, tried to make some sense of the figures, of the "arithmetic."

What seemed to be a final figure was blacked out, lead rubbed across it, the side of a pencil. I held it up to the sunlight, to see if the figure, made with the sharp lead of a pencil, could be made out under the softer lead rubbed over it.

And it could.

$1,000,000, it said.

I felt myself starting to shake. Something cold was coming up my spine, and it wasn't the air conditioning.

I began going through the desk drawers; among various bills and a few personal papers—including a drawing of this farmhouse in crayon signed "Mal" (which I did not draw, incidentally)—was a white form from the Port City Travel Agency.

It was a confirmation notice on a round-trip plane reservation for one, two weeks ago.

To Las Vegas.

17

"I DON'T BELIEVE THIS," JILL FOREST SAID, stepping out of the cab into the neon noon that was Las Vegas at midnight.

I handed the driver a ten-dollar bill and climbed out after Jill, saying, "Neither do I."

We were on Fremont Street, and above us a gigantic garish sign said 4 KINGS above neon versions of its playing card namesakes. The Four Kings was a hotel and casino, taking up a block of the casino center, a.k.a. Glitter Gulch, in downtown Las Vegas. Just across the way, and down the street, were the Horseshoe and the Golden Nugget and the rest, mammoth glowing tributes to Mammon. It was overwhelming, this carnival of craps got out-of-hand, this Disneyland of dollars. And here I was basking in it. Here *we* were.

"I don't think we're in Kansas anymore," Jill said. She had a large purse on a strap slung over her shoulder—it was serving as an overnight bag for both of us, actually—and her short red dress with wide patent-leather belt gave her a pop culture look that made her fit right in with the pulsating landscape. I was wearing a short-sleeve dark blue shirt that was sticking to me, and black slacks, and had a sportsjacket slung over my arm. Jane at Port City Travel had suggested I bring one along, despite the hundred-degrees-plus heat (and even at midnight, it was easily that); that way I'd look more presentable in the fancier casinos on the Strip, should we end up there. But it was also for comfort; as she (Jane) had pointed out, the casino air conditioning was on the chilly side; she knew people who'd fainted from going in and out of the Vegas cold and heat.

The conversation with Jane, incidentally, had been a hurried one this very afternoon. I had stopped in at Port City Travel, located in the Port City Hotel on Mississippi Drive, a little after three, having just got back from Ginnie's farmhouse where I'd run across that confirmation slip on her final Vegas trip. Jane, a pleasant-looking, cheerful brunette about my age—yet another old friend from high school, but a class behind us—told me she'd booked that trip; that she'd booked many such trips for Ginnie over the past ten years. Their high school connection had prompted Ginnie's doing business with Port City Travel, rather than an Iowa City agency, or so I supposed.

Anyway, Jane told me that Ginnie always stayed at the Four Kings, that she was friendly with the casino manager there, a man named Charlie Stone.

"What's really odd about *this* trip," Jane said, sitting at her desk by a little computer screen, "is it was for overnight."

"I noticed that," I said, "on the confirmation slip. And you find that odd?"

"Yes—for Ginnie, at least. Actually, sometimes we fly groups in for twenty-four-hour whirlwind junkets ... businessmen sometimes, college students especially get a real kick out of that sort of thing. But never Ginnie, not before this."

"How long would she usually stay in Vegas?"

"She'd go out for a week or ten days."

"What if I wanted to fly out there today?"

"Today? Las Vegas? Are you kidding?"

"No. I'd leave from Moline, right? When would that be, and when would I get there, and how much would it cost me?"

She started punching info up on her computer; I had several options. I had several departure times to choose from, ranging between four and seven o'clock, but any way you sliced it the bite would be in the six-hundred-buck range.

"Ouch," I said.

"If you had booked in advance, or as part of a group or junket or something . . . wait a minute. I may have something for you. . . ."

Twenty minutes later I was at Cablevision, where I found Jill in her office, talking to somebody on the phone. She looked at me with a curious smile, covering the mouthpiece, and I said, "Want to go to Las Vegas?"

"Sure," she said, perky. "When?"

I looked at my watch. "Ten minutes."

That knocked the perk out of her. She completed her phone conversation in thirty seconds or so, all the while looking at me with wide eyes. She hung up, and I said, "We should have time for you to stop at your apartment and pick up a toothbrush, change of underwear and a bathing suit. Maybe we have time for me to do that, too."

"What are you *talking* about?"

"Flight leaves at five fifty-five, but we ought to be there half an hour early, and it's three now, and it's forty-five minutes to the airport, so what do you say?"

"Well . . . I . . . yes."

Later, on the plane, she said, "I don't know if I understand how it is, or why it is, that I'm saving you money by coming along."

"You aren't saving me anything by coming along. I told you. It was just cheaper to buy two seats than one. A couple canceled out on this group deal just today, and we stepped in their shoes for four-hundred something. It was over six, otherwise."

"So I could just as easily have been an empty seat beside you?"

"Sure. But you look better in that red dress than the seat would."

She smiled a little. "You're crazy. It's a good thing I'm the boss where I work, or I could get fired for this."

"You'll only miss a day. We're coming back tomorrow afternoon."

A mechanical delay turned our hour layover in Chicago into a two-hour one, and it was almost midnight when we landed at McCarran International, where we passed through avenues of slot machines, lined up like shiny tombstones, on our way past the baggage area, where taxis waited.

Now here we were, standing before a twenty-some-story building that took up a city block, with an overhang all around, a neon-framed marquee promising the expected games of chance as well as twenty-four-hour restaurants and free souvenirs, with big plastic glowing neon playing cards interspersed occasionally—specifically, kings of hearts, clubs, spades, diamonds.

"Have you ever been to Vegas before?" I asked her.

"No," she said. "You?"

"Long, long time ago. I lost a hundred dollars here."

"You make it sound tragic," she said, with a little smile. "That's not so much, is it?"

"It was at the time; I was still in the

service. And it only took me about an hour to
do it."

"Somehow I don't think you were the first
serviceman to lose a hundred dollars in this
town."

"Maybe not," I said, the desert heat starting to get to me. "Shall we go in?"

"Let's," she said, and I slipped my arm in
hers, and we went in.

Like other downtown casinos, the Four
Kings was smaller than the "super" casinos
on the Strip, but it was massive just the
same. The decor was somewhere between
riverboat and New Orleans whorehouse (not
unlike the redecorated Port City Elks Club
Ginnie had scoffed at), and the dealers and
croupiers, predominantly male, were in white
frilled shirts with string ties, to match the
riverboat/Maverick decor; the waitresses were
dressed much the same, though with mini-
skirts and mesh stockings; the gaming-table
patrons, of which there was no shortage,
were casually dressed. We paused at a craps
table, a large affair longer than it was wide,
that took four men to run; some spectators
had gathered there, joining the players, and
we had to strain to see. Standing at one end,
a fat, fiftyish, balding, cigar-puffing guy in a
red and blue Hawaiian shirt and polyester
pants a shade of brown never dreamed of by
God was kissing the red plastic cubes and
their white dots; he then held the dice out
gingerly between thumb and forefinger like a
sacrament before the proferred pucker of a

stunning blonde of about twenty in a pink low-cut sweater and impossibly tight white jeans. She kissed the dice, neatly. He kissed her, sloppily. Then he flung the dice.

They bounced off the backboard, tumbled across the money-green felt awhile, came up 6 and 5.

"Aw *right*!" the obnoxious fat guy said, chewing on his stogie; the blonde cheerleader bounced up and down, only it was a stationary bounce: she went up and down like a piston, due perhaps to the tightness of her pants.

"Put your eyes back in your head, Mallory," Jill said, with a mock-nasty smirk.

"I've just never seen polyester that color before," I said.

"Right," she said. "How are you planning to find this guy Charlie Stone?"

"Let's ask at the check-in desk."

Which was on the abbreviated second floor, a balcony overlooking the casino's sea of green felt and the people swimming there. Since this package we'd lucked into was your basic twenty-four-hour crash-course in Vegas, hotel rooms weren't included—we'd crashed an all-night party, it seemed. But since we weren't here to party, I'd had Jane back at Port City Travel make us a hotel reservation. What I had to do in Vegas could be accomplished in a few hours tonight, and possibly a few more tomorrow. With luck. And if you couldn't get lucky in Las Vegas, where could you?

"Port City, Iowa," the middle-aged male clerk behind the counter said, with a knowing smile; he had a mustache and slick hair. "We'll make sure you get the special rate."

Jill and I exchanged bewildered looks.

"Why?" I asked, ever skeptical about gift horses.

The clerk beamed. "You're friends of Mr. Stone, aren't you?"

Aw *right*!

"And you didn't even kiss my dice," I said to Jill.

"Pardon?" the clerk said.

"Nothing," I said. "Is Charlie in?"

"Sure," the clerk said. "You know Charlie —he loves working nights."

"Actually," Jill said, "we don't know Charlie. We're just friends of a friend. We promised we'd say hello."

"Well," the clerk said with practiced cheer, "I'm sure that's no problem. Anybody from Port City is a friend of Charlie's."

And he called down to the casino floor and had Charlie Stone paged.

Soon a big, heavyset, white-haired, ruddy man in a sharkskin suit and a black silk tie was approaching us with a huge hand extended toward me and a smile as big as the neon cowboy's who loomed over Glitter Gulch.

"So you're from Port City!" he said. His eyes were casino-felt green, but a little red-lined; booze? "What's your name?"

I told him, and he snapped two thick fingers; the sound was like a gunshot.

"You're that mystery writer! I read about you in the paper."

Jill and I exchanged looks again. "What paper?" I asked. Had I made the Las Vegas *Sun*?

"Port City *Journal*, of course," he said. "I subscribe. Best way in the world to keep up—next to having friends drop by. And what's your name, miss?"

He had offered Jill his big hand—on one finger of which was a single large gold ring glittering with diamonds, his only ostentatious touch—and she was taking it, telling him her name.

"Was your father Fred J. Forest?"

"Yes!"

"Didn't he marry Viola Phillips?"

"That's my mother!" Then, as if apologizing: "But I'm afraid they've both passed away."

He patted her shoulder; like her long lost Uncle Charlie. "I'm sorry to hear that. I knew Fred pretty well. He was younger than me—wild kid, though!"

Jill smiled, a tinge of sadness in it. "He was a pretty sedate father. But I heard rumors he got around, way back when."

"That he did," Stone said, grinning broadly. "Can I get you folks a drink? Are my people treating you right?"

"I wouldn't mind a drink, actually," Jill said.

"Nor would I," I said. "And your people

are treating us fine. We're getting some sort
of special rate on our room."

He waved a thick hand in the air, magi-
cian like, diamond ring reflecting light. "More
special than that. We'll comp you."

"Well, thank you," I said. "That's hardly
necessary . . ."

"Not a word!" he said. "Let's go down to
my office and chat." He asked us what we'd
like to drink, and Jill wanted a Manhattan,
and after that dry air outside I wanted a
Pabst more than life in the hereafter, and he
had the check-in clerk make a call.

We went down the wide, rose-carpeted
steps and back into the casino, past a battal-
ion of chrome and glass slots, where patrons,
women mostly, stood worshipping, making
offerings, often from paper cups of coins,
staring at the brightly glowing colored glass
in the polished metal machines, transfixed
by spinning fruit. Beyond the slots were the
gaming tables—blackjack, craps, baccarat.
Then roulette, chuck-a-luck, wheel-of-fortune;
in a separate open room, with comfortable
chairs, armrests and all, people were playing
a bingolike game called keno. The air in here
was cold, and though many people were
smoking, not at all smoky; the room was
brightly lit, but despite the high ceiling, it
was something like being in a great big
submarine.

Stone led us through the casino—where
slightly muffled Dixieland music from a
lounge mingled with the ka-chunk of slot

machines eating money, their alarm bells signaling sporadic payoffs that came in rattling downpours of coin—and into a small, spartan office. Just a desk, some framed documents; a single black-and-white, wall-mounted TV monitor of an overview of the casino. It was a lot like Brennan's office, without the ducks.

A riverboat-gal waitress came in and delivered our drinks. We thanked her.

"So you're originally from Port City," I said. You didn't have to be a mystery writer to figure that one out.

"Born and bred," he nodded. He'd ordered a drink, too: milk. "Been in Nevada thirty years now. But I left Port City, oh, ten, fifteen years prior."

Jill smiled prettily and said, "How did a Port City boy wind up managing a casino?"

He laughed—a single booming "ha." "Day at a time, dear. Began running a crap game over a saloon in Port City, many, many years ago. Those were wild days."

I sipped my Pabst, smiled meaninglessly. "I hear Port City was pretty rough, back then."

"Yes sir, it was. Cooled down in the fifties. I moved on to Idaho when they legalized gambling, and finally wound up here—as a dealer, floor man, pit boss, shift boss. Worked my way up the ladder, like any business."

"Do you ever get back to Port City?"

"Not in years," he said, regretfully. "My family's died out, mostly—what little's left of 'em aren't in Port City anymore. But friends drop by. I keep in touch with, oh, dozens of people from home. I try to show 'em a good time, too."

"You knew Ginnie Mullens, then?"

His pleasant expression fell; the ruddy face looked longer than my day had been. With infinite sadness, he said, "She was a sweet kid. Mixed up, maybe. But I loved her."

"How did you happen to know her? She wasn't even *born* when you left town. . . ."

He held the glass of milk in one hand, looked into it, as if searching for memories. "I knew her dad. Jack Mullens." He glanced up, brightening. "*Great* guy! That guy coulda sold Satan a truckload of Bibles. He always had some damn scheme or other up his sleeve, some new idea that was gonna make his fortune. Never did, though. Poor guy. Died young, y'know."

"Not as young as Ginnie," I said.

"They were a lot alike," Stone said. He drank half the glass of milk, more or less; set it down, pushed it away, through with it, a duty he'd dispatched. Ulcers? He folded his hands before him, fingers thick as sausages. "I loved her old man. We played poker, shot craps, from dusk till dawn, many a time. He was younger than me, a little. But we had some wild ol' times. May he rest in peace."

"When and how did you get to know Ginnie?"

He thought back. "Well—it must've been twelve, thirteen years ago. She came out here, just turned twenty-one. Introduced herself. Cute as a button, smart as a whip. Spittin' image of her daddy. Pretty version of 'im. Wanted to work as a blackjack dealer. That wasn't unheard of; lots of college kids were getting jobs with us and other casinos, if they were of age and good enough. And she was. She handled the cards well. She knew the score. She knew the odds, too. Good little gambler, most of the time. Though she had a bad habit of . . ." He stopped.

"Taking risks?"

"Gambling at all's a risk. Life's a risk."

"So's playing in traffic."

"Well," he admitted, "you got something there—she'd play in traffic, sometimes. Take kinda pointless risks. Take long shots, and, well, hell, sometimes they pay off. Anybody involved in gambling over a long period of time knows never to rule out the improbable."

"They also learn never to rule out the probable."

"True," he said.

"You read about her death in the Port City *Journal*, then."

"Yes. I get it two days late. The paper. I got it today."

So that was why his eyes were red.

"It came as a shock to you," I said.

"It came as a disappointment. You can't work in this town for thirty years without losin' your sense of shock."

Jill sat forward. Said, "Ginnie's been coming here to gamble over the last ten years, hasn't she? Every now and then?"

He nodded. "She'd stay here, and gamble some here. But she was a smart cookie. She moved from casino to casino. Never winning too much. She was counting cards in black-jack when it was just a rumor." He laughed. "Same with baccarat. Those were her games. Y'know, she had the right kind of smarts, right kind of psychology. Most dealers are men, with your typical macho ideas and all. So she'd doll herself up—a low-cut sweater that showed off her frame, a slit skirt, some makeup ... she was a cute thing, anyway, that red hair of hers. And the men dealers just sit there grinning at her while she whips their butts and end up handing her thousands of dollars and then smile and help her to her taxi after. The male ego. Ha!"

"She usually did well?" I asked.

"Until the last year and a half or so. She had a real bad run of luck, took some major losses." He thought for a moment. "You know, it wasn't just that she caught a wrong-way streak, either—I don't think she was *playing* as well. She played the market some, too, you know, and I know she lost *plenty*, there."

"When she came to town, how long would she usually stay?"

"Like any good gambler," he said, "she knew that to make the odds work for you, you got to invest some time, as well as money. She'd give it ten days, usually."

"But this last time," Jill said, "she was only here a *day*...."

Sadness pulled at his face like a weight. "That was an unfortunate thing."

"Please explain," I said.

"Let me ask you something," he said. "Why are you here? Why do you want to know these things about little Ginnie?"

"I was her friend," I said. "I was her best friend, once. The sheriff ..."

"Brennan," Stone interrupted. "I knew his people."

"Yes; anyway, the sheriff has reason to believe Ginnie may have been murdered. The suicide seems to have been, well ... rigged."

"I see," Stone said, leaning forward; he was like a huge St. Bernard sitting upright in a chair. "So this is an ... inquiry of sorts?"

"Unofficial," I said. "I'm not a cop. Just a friend of Ginnie's. But the sheriff will hear what I find out."

"She played craps," he said.

"What?"

"This time ... this one time ... she played craps."

"I thought you said she was a blackjack and baccarat player, exclusively—"

"This *one time* she played craps." He sighed. "I blame myself. I okayed the thing. She'd have just gone somewhere else with it, if I didn't let her."

"What are you saying?"

Shaking his big head, with sadness, regret,

he said, "She came here with a satchel of money. $250,000. Cash. I told her, honey, you got a line of credit a block long here, and she said, no. Cash. She'd sold her business, y'see. She was here to break that losing streak of hers. And to play out a theory ... a pet theory of hers."

"Which was?"

He seemed almost embarrassed to say it. "Ginnie believed—and there's some truth to it—that your best odds are on your first bet. Your odds decrease as you stand and play. She always said that one day she wanted to walk in here and put her whole bankroll on one roll of the dice. One bet. One win.

"Or one loss," I said.

"Or one loss," he agreed.

"And did she?"

"Yes."

"And you allowed that?"

"If I hadn't, she coulda walked over to the Horseshoe. Or the Union Plaza. She wanted to gamble. And that's what we're in business for. All of us."

"Tell us what happened."

"She bet half of her satchel of money on herself, on the 'pass' line. She threw a ten. She bet the rest of her satchel of money on throwing a 'hard way' ten, which'd be two fives. Meaning if she made her point, if she shot a ten before crapping out, and shot a two-five ten doing it, she'd get eight-to-one odds on the second bet, *plus* even money on the original bet."

"I'm not sure I understand," I said.

"Well, with what she was betting, if everything worked out—over and above her original $250,000—she'd have made a cool million."

That figure again.

"And?" I asked.

He shrugged; them's the breaks.

"She crapped out," he said.

18

JILL WORE A WHITE BIKINI THAT WAS STAR-
tling against her brown skin; so was her
bright red lipstick. The short punky cut of
her black hair gave her beauty a nicely
casual quality. She was stretched out on her
back on a lounge chair, letting the hundred-
degree Nevada sun—almost directly over us—
beat down on her. Tiny beads of sweat
pearled her body. Sunglasses with sweeping
pink fifties-style frames shielded her eyes.
Occasionally she sipped a tall cool fruity
drink, the kind with an umbrella in it. I was
sitting nearby, on the edge of the pool, feet
dangling in the cool water. Cool compared to
the climate, that is. Half turning to look at
her, I realized she was the most beautiful
woman here, and there were plenty of youn-

ger, fleshier bikinied beauties around the
pool atop the Four Kings, showgirls some of
them, actresses, stewardesses, what-have-you.
But to my eyes Jill Forest, thirty-three, of
Port City, Iowa, topped them all.

I withdrew my legs from the pool and
walked over next to her and sat on a towel,
heat from cement coming right through and
scalding my ass. I didn't care. I wanted to
talk to Jill.

"Have you ever been married?" I asked
her.

A faint smile flickered over a face (a flaw-
less face, actually, but that would be one too
many *f*'s) that might otherwise have belonged to a sleeping beauty.

"Took you long enough to ask that question," she said, red lips barely moving, upper
lip moist with bodily dew.

"Maybe I was afraid to ask."

"Have *you* been married, Mal?"

"You know I haven't."

"Ever lived with anybody?"

"A couple times, when I was much younger."

"Funny."

"What's funny?"

An expression I couldn't read flitted across
her face before her features settled into that
expressionless tanning look. "You don't seem
the confirmed bachelor type."

"Sometimes bachelors my age are assumed
to be gay, you know."

She lifted a hand to the sunglasses, lowered them to peer at me archly for a mo-

ment. "You're not gay." Put the pink frames back in place.

"Glad you noticed."

Despite that show of confidence, the truth was we hadn't made love last night. It was one something A.M. when we finished talking to Charlie Stone, and we walked Glitter Gulch awhile, peeking in here and there, and then hired a cab to take us up the Strip, finally got out and walked some of that, taking in the neon and the kitschy decadence. Not a word was said about Ginnie the whole time. It was almost four when we finally drifted up to our hotel room, and tumbled into bed like dice and crapped out.

Then, when the sun sliced through the place where the drapes hadn't been closed all the way, I roused, aroused, drowsily rolled over and up against something or somebody and suddenly more or less realized a beautiful woman was in bed with me. Half asleep, not knowing who this woman was exactly, not remembering who I was exactly, I began cuddling, bumping, generally making trouble, and the beautiful woman responded, seeming pleasantly surprised to find a man in her bed, and, tangled in blankets and sheets, the musky smell of slumber on us both, we made love in that sweet, spontaneous, half-asleep, am-I-dreaming, quite wonderful way, and fell back asleep again, in each other's arms this time.

But we were up and about by nine-thirty, despite the late night before, and found a breakfast buffet and (taking Charlie Stone up on yet another offer of kindness) signed for our food, so that it would be attached to a bill we weren't being asked to pay.

We'd spent the rest of the morning around the pool; we'd both been in swimming, but mostly she sunned, I swam and (I suspect) we both stewed.

Because we hadn't yet mentioned Ginnie Mullens, or Charlie Stone's disclosures about her.

"Well?" I asked.

"Well what?" she replied, barely moving her lips.

"Have you ever been married?"

She took the sunglasses off, turned her head, looked right at me. The cornflower blue eyes in that dark face were a continual surprise. She shook her head ever so slightly, lovely face expressionless, and said, "No."

Then, just another shrewd Vegas gambler waiting for the other guy to make his mistake, she left the sunglasses off, looked at me; smiled a tiny, tiny smile, daring my response.

Which was, "Why not?"

"Because you broke my heart when I was a child." She said this straight-faced, with just a hint of humor.

"Oh, I did, did I?"

"You most certainly did."

"So, then, you probably never ever lived with anybody, either?"

Smiling more openly, she turned her head skyward, putting the sunglasses back on.

"Sure I did," she said. "Several times, over the years."

"This, after I broke your heart?"

Now her smile was wicked. "I'm a fast healer."

"Why didn't you marry any of the guys?"

The smile faded. "It just wasn't . . . right."

"As in 'Mr. Right'?"

She looked over at me; my reflection was in her sunglasses—my hair was wet from swimming, I noticed. "If," she said, "you're implying I've been waiting for *you*, Mr. Mallory, lo these many years, then your ego is even sicker than I think it is."

I didn't want to banter anymore; the tone of what I said next established that.

"Look," I said. "We're both the same age . . . well, I'm a little older. And I just wondered if . . ." I tried to think of a way to say this without insulting her; the best way seemed to be to leave her out of it, and stick to me. ". . . I wonder sometimes if life isn't slipping through my fingers. I'm at, or nearing, the probable halfway point of my life . . . assuming a truck or, as we say in Las Vegas, the 'big casino' or something doesn't knock me down first. And what do I have to show for my years on this planet?"

"You've written books," she offered.

"I've accomplished some things, I'll grant you. But I've been selfish. I spent my youth bumming around, doing this, doing that, building experience as a pool from which to write my stories. Fine—now I'm writing them and getting paid for the privilege, I've come up in the world, I have a house, a car, and the mortgage and payments that go with it. I've arrived. But where am I?"

"In the midst of the American dream, I'd say."

"Yeah, and sometimes I wish I could wake up. I'm like so many of my generation—all of us baby boomers, us selfish brats who were going to change the world and didn't. Haven't I ended up with the same values, the same materialistic trappings as my parents? Do you ever feel that way? Has that ever occurred to you?"

"Yes," she said.

"But our parents had something we don't, you and I. They had each other. They had a family. Have you ever had a child, Jill?"

She could've taken offense, but she didn't. "No," she said.

"Our generation put that off, you know. Women are waiting till they're in their late thirties now before having a kid, if at all. Careers. Self. That's us. But where's next year's model going to come from, Jill?"

"Are you . . . asking me to . . . ?"

"No. I'm not asking you to marry me, not yet anyway. I'm not even suggesting we live together. Not yet. But I want to go on record: if we're going to build some kind of . . . relationship—and Christ how I hate that word—I want it to be for real. I can't handle any more one-night stands, and if I ever find myself in a singles bar again I may climb a tower with a rifle and start shooting."

She was sitting on the edge of the lounge chair now. "What brought this on?"

"I don't know."

"Yes you do," she said wisely. "And so do I."

"Ginnie, I guess," I admitted reluctantly.

"Ginnie. Talented, brilliant, funny, pretty Ginnie. Gone. A life wasted."

"It wasn't a waste," I said. "There were good things in her life. And she left a sweet little child behind her, and that's something anyway."

Jill looked toward the shallow end of the pool where an attractive blonde mommy ten years younger than either of us romped with her three-year-old. "I've felt these things you're feeling, Mal. Maybe I've felt them more sharply than you. You don't have a biological clock ticking away in your tummy, do you? I'm thirty-three and if I want to have any children, maybe I better get cracking."

"Do you want to have children?"

"For a long, long time, I didn't think I did. These last couple years ... I'm not so sure." She looked at me, studying me, then bent down and gave me a kiss; not a sexy kiss, but a very affectionate one. "Let's not be a one-night stand, Mal. Or a two-night or anything less than giving ourselves a real chance."

"Agreed."

We shook hands.

My watch was on a towel on the other side
of her; I asked her to check the time.

"Half-past noon," she said.

"We don't have to leave for the airport till
four. Plenty of time to do some things. We
could do some sight-seeing, some shopping . . ."

"How about a few hours in our hotel
room?" The wicked smile again.

"I could be talked into that," I said, my
smile a little on the wicked side itself.

"Unless you'd rather gamble . . ."

"Coming here was all the gamble I care to
take."

"It paid off, didn't it?"

"Yes," I granted, "but I can't make sense
out of what I've learned; not yet, anyway."

"You're thinking that Ginnie is starting to
look like a real suicide."

I rubbed some sweat off my forehead;
sighed. "She sure seems to've been at the
end of her string. Her personal relationships
were a shambles. ETC.'s had been pulled out
from under her. You know, I asked her at the
reunion how business was, and she said
'good'—but that was *after* the ETC.'s sale.
Her only business at that point was dope.
She was really at a dead end . . . the only
thing she still had going for her was playing
mule for Sturm—and there could hardly
have been much satisfaction in that for someone of Ginnie's abilities and ambitions."

"What about her recent obsession with the

past?" Jill said. "She talked to me about the 'good old days' for hours. Then she came back to Port City for that reunion, looked up her old boyfriend, tried to get something going with him, fifteen years later."

"A pretty desperate move," I said. "Hardly rational, considering how little she and Faulkner had in common at this point."

"Maybe she wasn't finding any answers in the present, and hoped to find them in the past."

A teenage boy and girl were splashing in the deep end nearby, making happy noise.

"Maybe," I nodded. "At the reunion she was talking about her old goal of making a million by the time she was thirty—she was a few years past thirty, but hadn't given up the goal. She just 'adjusted' it."

"That's why she came here," Jill said, meaning Las Vegas. "To go for broke. A last ditch effort—"

"Make a quick kill," I agreed.

"Sad." Jill shook her head, black hair tumbling; put her towel around her shoulders. "To take all she had and throw the dice. All that money from selling the business she'd built up with years of hard work—a roll of the dice, and gone."

"That's what bothers me most," I said.

"What?"

"She got $100,000 out of the ETC.'s sellout, right?"

"Yes . . ."

"Well, Charlie Stone said she lost $250,000 at the craps table."

She touched fingertips to lipsticked lips. "I hadn't thought of that—"

"Exactly. Where'd she get the other $150,000?"

19

AT THE HOTEL ROOM A RED LIGHT WAS LIT ON the phone, indicating I had a message; I called down to the desk—I was to call Charlie Stone, at his home number, which they gave me. I tried several times, but there was no answer. Finally, shortly before we should be leaving for the airport, I tried one last time. And this time he did answer.

"Mr. Stone!" I said. "Thank you for all you've done...."

"I'm going to do you one more favor," he said, his voice soft, strong. "I'm going to tell you something else about Ginnie Mullens—something I'd have to deny should anybody official ask me."

I swallowed. "Understood."

"I held back from you last night. I had to sleep on it."

"Okay."

Pause.

Then: "I had a phone call last week from someone in Chicago. The name wouldn't mean anything to you, but I'm not going to mention it, just the same." Another pause. "Questions were asked about Ginnie."

"Questions . . . ?"

"About what happened in this casino two weeks ago. And whether or not she was a high roller, a regular here, which of course she was." His voice took on a weary note of resignation: "They asked, and I told it like it is, with her—or anyway, like it was. Y'see, when certain people ask, there's no choice but to answer."

I didn't know what to say to that; I could hear him breathing on the other end of the line.

"You should also consider," he said finally, "that if I got a call, so did other people around town."

"What do you make of that?"

"Certain business interests in Chicago were checking up on Ginnie not long before she died."

"What does that mean?"

"I got no idea," he said; he seemed to be telling the truth. "Why anybody in Chicago would have the slightest interest in Jack Mullens's little girl is beyond me."

"Did you tell Ginnie about this? Did you call her and warn her?"

"Warn her of what?"

"Did you call her, Mr. Stone?"

"Subject closed."

"Mr. Stone . . ."

"I hope you enjoyed your stay at the Four Kings."

The line went dead.

Jill had come in halfway through the call to sit on the edge of the bed, in a towel, having just showered, brushing her hair.

"What was that all about?" she asked, eyes wide and blue.

"It was the piece of information I've been looking for," I said.

"Oh?"

"Yeah. Hurry up and get your clothes on, or we'll miss our plane. Don't take anything to read—we'll have plenty to talk about."

"Such as?"

"Such as who killed Ginnie, and why."

"Do you know?"

"I know."

20

CURTAINS HAD CLOSED THE EYES IN THE JACK-o'-lantern face of the Frank Lloyd Wright-style barn in which Marlon H. Sturms dwelled. Amber street lights lit the classy housing development, giving this street, which lawyers and doctors shared with a dope dealer, a cool unreality; traffic was nil, the only sign of life the lights behind certain windows in certain houses, including the uppermost two eyes of the jack-o'-lantern, their curtains glowing a soft yellow.

It was a few minutes past midnight, and Jill and I were sitting in my Firebird, having pulled inconspicuously (we hoped) into the driveway of a house whose windows were all dark, on the opposite side of the street from Sturms, down a third of a block or so. We'd arrived back at Moline around ten forty-five, and got right on Interstate 80 and come straight to Iowa City.

I was a little nervous, but also felt a certain high. Which seemed fitting somehow.

Jill said she was nervous, too, but seemed at ease; I hoped the opposite wasn't true of me.

"You know what to do?" I asked.

She nodded, patted my arm supportively.

I got out of the car, crossed the street, went up the walk, taking its four gentle jogs, the antique farm implements displayed in the front yard looking in the light of night like so much junk, and since it had been paid for by junk, why not?

I pressed the doorbell, heard it play its unrecognizable tune.

No one answered.

I tried again. And again. And again and again.

Finally a voice behind the door, a tenor voice that no longer seemed bored, said: "What in hell is it?"

"It's Mallory," I said.

"Go away!"

"I just want to talk to you."

"Go to hell!"

Sturms didn't seem his usual cool self tonight.

"I can talk to you," I said, "or the police."

Silence.

Then the door cracked open, and a slice of Sturms's face with one of his eyes stuck in it peered out at me over the night latch. His wife had greeted me the same way once, only she was pretty, and not as paranoid.

"Talk," he said.

"Inside," I said, gesturing.

"Talk here, or go to hell."

"Inside," I repeated. "In this neighborhood I might attract attention, standing here like this. On the other hand, if you'd like to risk my explaining to the first patrol car that comes along why I dropped by to see you tonight, well . . ."

The door shut momentarily, the night latch was undone and he opened the door for me. Not thrilled about it. Did I mention he had a gun in his hand? A small square blue automatic.

In addition to the gun, he wore a white short-sleeved sportshirt with an alligator on it, gray slacks, and a haggard face. Though it was cold in the house, sweat beaded the broad, flat nose, his only irregular feature.

The living room was dark, but for a few small museum-style lights on the nearer side of the room, under various examples of his wife's unique style of abstract painting; her canvases on the walls served as constant exclamation points in the otherwise under-stated sentence of this living room. The detached, modern furnishings were all wrong for the panicked look in Sturms's eyes, which made the berserk abstractions of his wife's paintings seem unintentionally apt represen-tations of what must be going on in the man's mind about now. Having such a man point a gun at you could be unsettling. And unsettled I was, but not afraid. This man was defeated already.

"Going somewhere?" I asked, nodding toward the two tan travel bags and one suit carrier that were sitting near the door I'd just come in.

"Is that your business?" Never were four so simple words vested with such quiet hysteria.

"I think so. Don't point that at me."

He lowered the gun a bit.

I gestured to a beige burlap modular sofa nearby; one of his wife's paintings loomed above it, a patriotic theme: red slash, blue slash, on white.

We sat. The sofa was very soft, but not particularly comfortable; Sturms sat forward, the gun in hand dangling between his legs.

"What do you want?" he said. The hysteria level was lower now, letting his fatigue show through. The bags by the front door were nothing to those under his eyes—this guy hadn't slept for a while.

"Just to talk," I said.

"Talk, then."

"When are you leaving?"

"Tomorrow morning. First flight out, from Cedar Rapids. Why?"

"Just asking."

"Never mind where!"

"Okay, okay. Take it easy, Sturms. I'm not the cops."

He laughed, darkly. "Cops are the least of my worries."

"I suspected as much. When did they tell you?"

He glanced at me warily. "Tell me what?"

"That you were being cut off. When did Chicago tell you you were through?

He almost winced at that. He was looking at the gun in his hand when he said, "This afternoon. I . . . I got the vibes before that. I sent my wife to her folks yesterday. I hope she'll be okay. Maybe . . . maybe I should just get in the car and go, hell with waiting till tomorrow."

"You think you're in danger?"

"I don't know. I don't know. I just know I'm out of the business." He looked at me imploringly. "They wouldn't take me out just 'cause of what I know?" Then his face fell. "Sure they would."

"They might," I admitted.

"I'm going now." He stood. "Hell with waiting for my flight."

I touched his arm—gently. He did have a gun. Not a big gun, perhaps, but how big did it have to be?

And he was pointing it at me again, looking at me sharply. "I got no time for this, Mallory."

"Settle down, settle down. If they were planning to do you in, why would they bother cutting you off first? Wouldn't they be more likely to pretend everything was as usual, if they were planning something?"

He thought about that; something like a smile formed under his flat nose. "You could be right. That does make sense."

"You can spare me a few minutes of talk."

"All right." He sat back down. "But then you're out of here."

"Fine."

"So talk."

"Do you have any money in those suit-cases?"

"What do you mean?"

"Because I'm going to tell you a story. And after you hear it, I think you may want to offer me some money not to tell anybody else." Pretending blackmail seemed the best way to get this wound opened back up.

Eyes wide, nostrils flared, teeth bared, the once cool Mr. Sturms was just another animal now. He said, "What's to stop me from killing you where you sit?"

"You'll spoil your fancy couch. Besides, I'm a writer. I may have written my story down, where someone might see it, should any accident befall me. You're an insurance man. You know all about accidents."

The gun in his hand was shaking now; I didn't much like that. But then he didn't much like me: "Tell me your goddamn story, then."

"All right," I said. "Here's my latest plot: a certain dope dealer, let's call him 'you,' has a faithful mule, let's call her Ginnie. Not long ago, the dope dealer gives his faithful mule

$150,000 to buy coke—only she never made the buy."

Hearing the $150,000, Sturms sucked in a breath. "How did you . . . ?"

"Come up with that figure? Ginnie packed a satchel full of cash, to make her last-ditch effort to break her Vegas losing streak. Actually, her losing streak extended to almost every other facet of her life as well, but never mind. Anyway, she took a quarter of a million with her—only, where did she get it?"

"She sold her store . . ."

"She only got a hundred grand for that."

He shrugged, unconvincingly. "She's been successful in business for years; she made a mint off of ETC.'s. . . ."

"No," I said. "She started small and grew; she socked most of her dough back in the business, and then when the money did start to roll in, she started draining the business to gamble. That's one of the reasons Caroline Westin dropped her."

"She made plenty working with me, Mallory—"

"I'm sure she did. I don't know how much mules make these days, but I'm sure you were generous. And I don't know where her money went, exactly. Some of it went up her nose, maybe. I do know in recent months she was broke. She'd been losing at Vegas, losing on the stock market; she took ten grand from her boyfriend, Flater, to gamble some more, then couldn't pay him back. She was busted,

Sturms. The money from the sale of the business was all she had. So, *where did she get the extra $150,000?*"

He blinked.

"From you" I said. "You gave her $150,000 to buy coke. And then instead she put it down on the pass line and threw the dice. And lost."

He was looking into the darkness across the room when he said, "I didn't kill her. I didn't have her killed, either."

"As good as. You told Chicago what she'd done."

He seemed genuinely sad. "I had no choice."

"You knew they'd take steps...."

"I had no choice."

"Chicago sent a man—I may have met him, in my kitchen the other night—and he entered Ginnie's house, quietly, and he killed her. And he made it look like suicide."

A muscle in his jaw jumped.

"Is that standard procedure?" I asked. "Faking hits to look like an accident, or suicide? Or had you requested it?"

He was looking at the gun in his hand.

"Ginnie hadn't counted on that," I said. "She hadn't counted on the hitman staging a phony suicide. That wasn't in her plans."

"Stop, Mallory. Please stop."

"Ginnie *did* commit suicide, in a way. A very real way."

"Please."

"She had taken one last gamble in her attempt to achieve her childhood goal—

millionaire by thirty ... well, give or take a few years. She had bet her life—using Chicago money."

"Please stop."

"And she lost. But like any good gambler, she had an ace in the hole: the insurance policies. When she lost at Vegas, she went back home to Iowa to wait for the inevitable. She knew that some angel of death, Chicago-style, would come around. So she sat and waited for something she wanted but couldn't quite bring herself to do. Knowing that those insurance policies would be there for her daughter—and Ginnie would achieve through her 'murder,' through her death, her life's goal. She'd make a million."

The gun clunked to the floor; he cupped his face with one hand and wept.

"You really were friends," I said, a little surprised, you and Ginnie. You really did like each other."

"We ... were lovers, once."

Ginnie'd had a few of those.

I said, "I'm not surprised Chicago's upset with you. That $150,000 Ginnie lost was your responsibility. They checked up on you last week, you know. They called around to the Vegas casinos. They discovered that Ginnie was a high roller, a gambler. They discovered that you had been using this gambler as a mule, had been entrusting their money, their thousands upon thousands of dollars, to this unreliable young woman in whom gambling was a sickness. By now they've discovered that you, in your insurance man mode, sold that same young woman a million dollars worth of policies, which guaranteed her death being looked into hard, by top-flight investigators. I'll bet you neglected to mention that when you called them to report Ginnie, the call that cost her her life. Your judgment must be looking pretty poor to the boys in Chicago about now."

He was staring at me with wide, angry eyes, but his shock was greater than his anger, and his fear was greater than his shock. On wobbly legs, he stood.

"I have to get out of here," he said.

"Maybe you should at that," I said.

A figure stepped from the darkness across the room and said, "Too late," and a silenced automatic *snicked* three times, making three little puffs across Sturms's chest, one getting him right in the alligator, and he jerked like a puppet, this way, then that, and slammed into his wife's painting, and slid down, leaving another slash of red on the painting, a more vivid red, a wetter red, that gave the painting a sudden clarity, made it suddenly make sense, and then I was sitting next to a corpse, whose empty eyes looked at me without looking at me.

The little blue automatic was on the floor.

The figure stepped even closer.

He was a big man in black in a ski mask. Which he now pulled off, revealing himself to me (and this was no surprise, though a shock nonetheless) as my friend from the kitchen, James C. Novack.

Who said, "Well. Looks like this is happy hour. Double bubble."

He was pointing the gun at me when the front door splintered as Detective Evans kicked it in; there was more splintering as the big man in black fired his silenced gun toward that door, but the sound of an unsilenced weapon filled the room and lifted the man in the air, cutting through his midsection, severing his spine, a burst of bone and blood and other matter flying out what had been his back, and he landed in a twisted sack of flesh that could only belong to a dead man.

I don't remember getting outside, but I did, as I do remember standing on the front lawn, near the antique farm implements, holding Jill in my arms, or rather she was holding me. My heart was pounding.

"I saw him sneaking around the side of the house," Jill said, breathlessly, meaning the dead guy in black, Novack. I'd told her that at the sight or sound of anything unusual, she was to find a phone quick and call Evans.

Evans stood on the porch, the splintered doorway behind him. He was sliding a huge revolver into a holster on his hip; it was the first time I'd seen him with a gun.

He said, "How are you doing?"

"Breathing," I said. "Thanks to you."

"I'll give you a while to get yourself together," he said. "I'm going to call Brennan and see if he can get right up here, and maybe round up a D.C.I. guy, too." He gestured with a thumb back toward the room beyond the splinterd door, where carnage waited. "Then you're going have to start explaining this."

"Okay," I said.

Jill held me.

She said, "Mal—you're *smiling*."

"I was just thinking," I said.

"What?"

"Ginnie's little girl is a millionaire."

21

ONE AFTERNOON THAT AUGUST, I WAS FIN-
ishing up a chapter on the new book when
someone knocked on my door. It turned out
to be Ginnie's mother, with a big cardboard
box in her arms. Roger was behind the wheel
of their new-model Buick with the engine
going, windows up, air conditioning on.

"Mrs. Mullens," I said, holding open the
screen door.

"Here," she said, smiling, handing me the
box; it was heavy. "I've been meaning to
drop these off."

"Won't you step in?"

"Just for a moment," she said, smoothing
the front of her cheery blue and white floral
dress. "Roger is waiting."

Bless his heart.

She stepped in, and I put the box down and said, "What's this, anyway?"

"Some books Ginnie left to you," her mother said. "Her will was very specific about who got what."

"You did come out pretty well, though?"

"Oh, yes," she said, smiling but not entirely meaning it. "Of course, there was a . . . codicil, I think it's called . . . requiring the estate to repay a debt."

"I know it's none of my business," I said, "but would that happen to have been $10,000, to a David F. Flater?"

"Why, yes, it was. How did you know that?"

"Your daughter and I were friends, Mrs. Mullens," I said, as if that explained it.

"Yes, you most certainly were." She touched my arm. "I really did love my little girl, you know."

"I know you did."

"As a mother myself, I should have known Ginnie wouldn't leave her own daughter unremembered."

With Ginnie's death now on the books as a murder, little Malinda was indeed a millionaire; it had taken the edge off Mrs. Mullens's notion that her daughter had left everything to her, to belatedly prove her love.

"Well," she said, smiling tightly, "I must run." She pecked my cheek, and I thought I detected the fragrance of 90-proof perfume.

Then she waddled down the stairs and drove off into the afternoon with her darling boy.

I went immediately back to work, and it wasn't till later that evening, when Jill dropped by for a drink, that I cracked open the box of books to see what Ginnie had left me.

Mostly they were books I'd given her. Hammett, Chandler, Cain, Spillane. Several tattered Roscoe Kane paperbacks. Willard Motley's *Knock On Any Door*, a hardcover first edition with dust jacket. I remembered the famous line from that book that Ginnie had quoted at our class reunion: "Live fast, die young, and have a good-looking corpse." I picked it up, to thumb through, and a folded slip of paper fell out.

I opened it up and read it.

It said, only, "Mal—forgive me."

Signed, of course, "Ginnie."

Dated the night of her death.

I showed it to Jill and she said nothing; a little later we walked outside to look at the river in the moonlight, the barge lights winking along it, the moon reflecting. The sky was black velvet with silver stars. I stared up at them.

"So she left a note, after all," Jill said.

"It might not have been meant for me," I said. "Her daughter's name is Mal, too, you know."

"It was meant for you. I think she was asking you to forgive her for what she said in the cafeteria that time."

"I forgave her that, a long, long time ago."
Jill shook her head. "Not really."

I put my arm around Jill's waist and I looked up at the stars.

"That's better," Jill said, and we went inside.